I BELIEVE

by ALAN LINDGREN

POETRY

The Seeker (1986)
O Days Are Made of Riddles (1987)
The Sun Sings / WORD-PICTURES 1997 (1999)
Winter Hymns (1997-1998)
Pulsing Love and Light Eternal (1998)
Sun and Moon and Stars of Night (1998)
Summer Songs (1998)
Autumn Harvest (1998)
The Diary (1999)
Instrument of the Poetic Word (1999)
A Poet's World (1999)
Ego and Love (1999)
Night-Mysteries 2004–2005 (2005)
Sun, Sparrow, and Star: Sacred and Secular Songs; Selected Poems (2009)
Journeying with the Sun: An Evolving Imagination; A Poetry Chronology (2013)

POETRY with ESSAYS and SHORT FICTION

Balance is Freedom and Freedom is Love (2002)
By the Sunset there's a Door (2002)
The Courage of the Flame (Two Editions) (2003)
The Magic of the Stars (Two Editions) (2004) (2005)
LOVE-PICTURES 2003–2005 (2005)
The Tides of Evening (Two Editions) (2006)
Love Was All He Vowed (2006)
Imagination: The Final Poems (Two Editions) (2006) (2007)
Imagination and Insight: Selected Poems and Essays (2007)
LIGHT-LICHT: Selected Poems with Three Essays (2007)

SHORT FICTION, PLAYS, a LIBRETTO, a TREATISE and a NOVEL

Regrouping in Idea and Practice, A Treatise on Mars (2007)
Fiction and Fact: Tales, Stories, and an Essay (2007)
The Folk Tale of the Two Tom-Tom Bird Cousins (2008)
Two Folk Tales 2008 (2008)
Michael and Los Angeles /A Novel (2008)
Oliver and Nancy / A Humorous Story in Ten Chapters (2009)
Two Short Plays by Alan Lindgren (2010) (2011)
Saltiff Shore – Where Love's Requited / A Comedy in Six Acts (2010)
The Property / A Play in Three Acts (2010)
Kings & Commoners, Mouse, Magic and More / Stories and Tales (2011)
Sons and Daughters / An Operetta in Prologue and Five Acts / The Libretto (2012)
I Believe, an Imagination with Tales and Stories by Alan Lindgren (2013)

BIOGRAPHY

Margaret Lindgren: A Biography and Picture of the Human Being (2005)
Alan's Life-Story (Two Editions) (2005)
The Life of Paul Stanley McLester (2006)
Arne Ragnar Lindgren: Man of Heart, Hand and Mind (2006)
Disa Ellen Lindgren: A Biography of a Modern Human Being (2006)

Alan Lindgren

I Believe,

an Imagination

with Tales and Stories

℘

Sun Sings Publications
Culver City

Alan Lindgren is an expert on the four temperaments and a much-published lyric poet, essayist, and fiction writer. He is the author of By the Sunset there's a Door: Poetry, Prose and Essays Celebrating Nature and Humanity, The Courage of the Flame: Ballads, Sonnets and Other Gardens of Poetry with Prose Writings, The Magic of the Stars: Poems 2003–2004, Sun, Sparrow, and Star: Selected Poems, and Journeying with the Sun: A Poetry Chronology. His fiction, articles, and poetry have appeared in *Biodynamics*, a publication of the *Bio-Dynamic Farming and Gardening Association, Inc.*, *The Correspondence*, newsletter of the Central Region of the Anthroposophical Society in America, and Highland Hall Waldorf School's newsletter *Rhythms*.

I Believe, an Imagination
with Tales and Stories by Alan Lindgren

Sun Sings Publications, Culver City, CA 90232
© 2013 by Alan Lindgren
All rights reserved. Published 2013.
Printed in the United States of America
Book design by Alan Lindgren
10 9 8 7 6 5 4 3 2 1

Library of Congress Control Number: 2013943966

1. An Imagination and Short Fiction. 2. Folk Tales. 3. Fairy Tales.
4. An Imagination. 5. Short Stories. 6. Tales. 7. Stories.
8. Brief Prose Sketches. 9. Gem Miniatures. 10. Short Fiction.
I. Title

Lindgren, Alan, b. 1962
[Tales and Stories/Short Fiction]
I believe, an imagination
with tales and stories/Alan Lindgren.–1st ed.
p.   cm.
ISBN: 978-0-9832053-5-7
2013

Acknowledgements

My special thanks to Judith Jaeckel, who selflessly supported the early publishing of my short fiction, and my poetry and essays at the time, and who connected me in a beautiful manner with Mountain Laurel Waldorf School in New Paltz, NY. My deep thanks to my best and dearest friends Dr. Virginia Sease and John Alexandra for their loyal encouragement, support, and great good will, heartfelt understanding and love, and precious friendships, which mean so much to me. With deepest gratitude I think on my dearest Christ-brother Gérard Klockenbring† (1921–2004), the great French Christian Community seminary principal and pastor-priest. My warmest gratitude and humanity for my dear and wonderful parents, Arne† (1918–1994) and Margaret Lindgren, who have supported me with unending patience and kindness, generosity and understanding, and faithful and loving hearts, since the earliest beginnings of my life through the present time—my 51-year journey on earth—full of human goodness and warmth. I owe so much especially to these human beings, and others too numerous to mention, that my heart is very full.

Friend of Michaél

Friend of Michaél, Friend of God
Think in radiant thoughts the Word
With His courage feel in hearts
Know His strength in wills imparts.

Man is human, Man becomes
Being balanced walking comes
Between lightness up above
And the weighted Earth find love

With thy hearts in bravery
Thoughts of Christ in freedom see
Thoughts of hearts courageously
Stream in sunlight's clarity

Learn thy willing discipline
In thy feeling sainthood win
Follow Christ in Michaél
Banish darkness, Sun prevail.

Alan Lindgren
Los Angeles
July 6, 2013

Contents

First-published *(for Youth and Adults)*

Republished

x

Preface

These past three weeks I have written three short prose pieces, partially fiction (one—*The Good King and the Wise Princess*—pure fiction, one—*The Forest*—a great aspect of history clothed in imagery in a brief story, the third—*I Believe*—an imagination that therefore lives in the spiritual world where it is a reality), unbidden. So this writing was entirely spontaneous on my part, as is my poetry composition, but it is lawful in form. Indeed *The Forest* is a poem in rhythm and rhyme, almost from the beginning, and the imagination (*I Believe*) consists mainly in single, inwardly-connected poetic images. I am a poet, so this is unsurprising. *The Good King and the Wise Princess* is, as noted in the contents, a classic fairy tale with a twist. Without giving it away, it really is a classic fairy tale in every other respect. So the form of this tale is also lawful, which means it is written on the pattern of all fairy tales. *Anna*, the fourth prose piece, and a short story published here for the first time, was written in October 2011. It is a well-written story, harmonious and nice. Both of these stories arose spontaneously as well.

For three-and-one-half years (since December 2009), I have devoted much thought, will, and time to write a major work of non-fiction, *Motifs in Human Life: Paths of Progress and Contribution; Studies in the Content of the World*. Because of its scope, if published this work would have to appear in a series of two or more sizeable volumes. It has undergone many changes, including different titles, subtitles, prefaces, and introductions, not to mention heavy revision and editing. But it is still far from completion; it is much too long; there is simply too much material. (If published as is it would take up at least 1200, 6" X 9" pages.) Yet the rewrites and a good portion of the rest are very well written and should be left intact. The actual studies are excellent. All of it I find of real interest, so that readers may find it interesting and helpful as well, else I would not have written it. But a good portion of it needs a serious pruning, to give an apropos analogy. I have written and published much in the interim. (*See* by A L A N L I N D G R E N, *beginning* (2010))

When yesterday the thought occurred to me I might publish a new book of my short fiction, selected from my work published in 2011 and earlier, and including the four pieces discussed above, I felt inspired that something entirely spontaneous in character is near at hand. (But for *Anna* and *The Good King and the Wise Princess*, the short fiction is previously published, but none of it is bogged down as some of *Motifs in Human Life*, rather it has freshness of composition. There are four other new prose pieces as well.*) Especially the genuine imagination of the title (*I Believe*) is behind this publication, which you may find on reading it. This imagination by itself makes publication worthwhile. It should be read aloud artistically as in the art of speech formation.

So it is I began work on the file, selecting the tales and stories from my previously published work, beginning the table of contents, writing the introduction, and choosing a title. It will be some time before the interior and cover files are ready for the printer, the distribution network is created, and the funds are raised, but the project has been born and is underway. And, knowing me, the computer work will be accomplished without delay or break, because when I set out to do something, it is good as done.

May this suffice to preface *I Believe, an Imagination with Tales and Stories by Alan Lindgren.*

Alan Lindgren
Los Angeles
June 23, 2013

* Note: *The Sunset—A Meditation in Prose* was written on July 7 and *Time—An Elegy* on July 13, 2013, and were added to the e-manuscript for eventual publication as the author felt they are significant. They are the fifth and sixth first-published pieces in this book, if one excludes the frontispiece, the poem *Friend of Michaél*, written on July 6, 2013. (St. Michael is an Archangel and the mighty Time-Spirit of our Age. The fiery Prince of Thought and the countenance of Christ (Rudolf Steiner), Michael is also the Archangel (Regent) of the Sun.)

Introduction

I wrote the short story *Anna* in 2011 shortly after my volume of short fiction, *Kings & Commoners, Mouse, Magic and More*, appeared in print, and I had always wanted to see it published. Now that I have written several other prose pieces, I thought there is the possibility to publish another volume of short fiction. In it, I republish the finest of my earlier short fiction work. This includes two of my fairy tales, five of my folk tales, a story for three to six-year-olds, seven various stories, four brief prose sketches, and two gem miniatures. This is the result.

I ask that you read *The Forest* and *I Believe (an Imagination)*, both published here for the first time, with special attention. They are, each in its own way, unique. *The Forest* is magical and true. In this it is like a fairy tale. In rhyming rhythms, which begin a few sentences into the piece, it is a poem. In content it is Christianity, past, present, future. The element of magic in *The Forest* is in its images created with a minimum of words. I was inspired when I wrote it, from when I took up the pen through writing down the last word. I did not pause. In this it is like my poems. But its magic in the word-pictures inspired me as I wrote it. This magic is of the faerie race of men, women, and children, as Mary the Mother ("Marie"), Jesus ("Jesu"), and John are of faerie. Many other human beings throughout history are of the faerie race (the Venus destinies), for example Adam, Elijah, Joan of Arc, M. L. King, and Peace Pilgrim. (*Time* is elegiac. *The Sunset* concerns reincarnation and karma, with perfection and initiation through earthly life.)

I Believe (an Imagination) is remarkable. In content it is soul-spiritual feeling, thinking, light, shadow, color, love, and warmth. In imagery it is a series of poetic pictures that, taken together, build up one large imagination. It is these poetic images, spoken, that have the power—at times moving, at times bright, at times pale and weak, at times colorful and tender, at the end strong in warmth, depth, and meaning—to stir intuitions in the reader's soul. A genuine imagination such as this is not what separate images or concepts are; it is a living creative being or picture that has existence in the spiritual world. Thus *I Believe* is no ordinary artistic creation. *I Believe* was written in clear, distinct, and concise word-sequences, for speech, with short breaks between. So it was written intentionally. But each subsequent sequence or image proceeds out of the previous one. This is the whole, a single spiritual imagination that arose from the inwardly connected individual word-pictures (poetic images). As with my poems, I did not know what I would write next as I put it down on paper. In this it is spontaneous. But because each word-picture proceeds out of the previous one, it is a lawful whole. Nothing is arbitrary. *I Believe* is a genuine imagination. The form is required within which the word-pictures live in inner necessity which is freedom. It should be artistically spoken as in the art of creative speech. The imagination entire is a spiritual reality. *I Believe* has existence in the spiritual world because it is a genuine imagination. It lives there for the reader or listener where it can be experienced. (See *I Believe (An Imagination)–A Brief Study*, next two pages)

****

I am a gifted folk tale writer; five are here published. The folk tale is a genre that communicates equally well, at different levels, to adult and child. Children have an authentic understanding of folk tales, because the lessons of the story are related in a simple narrative with down-to-earth characters at a slow pace. They see themselves and their peers directly in the characters and their interactions. Not only do they learn the lessons of the tale, they enjoy doing the same.

Adults understand folk tales and the same aspects, but from another perspective as they see through the characters to their human natures, and other aspects of human life as well, such as (folk) wisdom, responsibility, honesty, patience, the value of work, the priceless nature of handwork—many human traits, vices, and virtues. These qualities, spun into the timeless folk tale fabric, make these stories ideal for the classroom, especially for Grades One, Two, and Three. *The Folk Tale of the Baking Potato Farmer* was used in Ms. Tree Anne McEnery's Third Grade class for their Harvest & Measurements main lesson block in Mountain Laurel Waldorf School during the autumn of 2006.

Alan Lindgren

I Believe (an Imagination)
A Brief Study

Just as some pictures or imagery in a poem, a fairy tale, and some novels represent living spiritual realities who have existence in the spiritual world, which belong to the human soul in a special way, so does my imagination, *I Believe*, represent a living spiritual reality; it is a spiritual imagination that has existence in the spiritual world where it can be perceived with the eyes of the soul, which therefore belongs to the human soul in a special manner. This living imaginative reality of a supersensory nature is clear and necessarily deep, because it springs from my heart and soul, from my indwelling spirit (the divine within me), my inner source, my source of soul light, comparable to the Sun and sunlight of the heavens.

Because each human being has the possibility to connect the spirit within to the divine individualized in a drop in each one of us, every sensitive and open human mind, soul, and heart may experience my imagination, thus communicating genuine understanding of its living spiritual content to the English-language reader.

Because of the nature, qualities, and power of spoken language, of that which is inherent in speech, it is best for my imagination to be spoken artistically as in the art of speech formation (creative speech). Only then will the inwardly connected single images or pictures, each to the preceding one, and therewith the entire imagination, give their full, living expression. Language rightly spoken creating lives with spiritual fire, inner mobility, forming, shaping, sounds, light and shadows, colors, pictures, rhythms, rising and falling, movement, depths, breadths, heights, elasticity, condensing, quickening—entire worlds—while text that is read in silence cannot live in the same way, however poetic or beautiful.

In my brief imagination, what is called *belief* is actually *experience* in the deeper sense of the word. This is soul and heart experience. The rest follows, but in a natural, which is to say living progression. The single pictures or images, which are inwardly connected, one out from within the preceding one, reveal experiences of a soul nature. If one lives in these purely inner experiences in the right way, the images (poetic pictures that are spiritual) are actually seen and felt by the soul and heart of the reader, speaker, or listener. The light, shadows (grey rose petals), colors, little flower-blossoms, are soul-light, soul shadows (soul grey rose petals), soul colors, soul little flower-blossoms, the warmth soul-spiritual, the Sun spiritual. Because my imagination is clear and warm (moral, good) as the sunlight we revere is clear and warm (moral, good), the word-pictures are pure. But the sunlight is also beautiful, and the fact that I am a poet brings these qualities into poetic, which is to say beautiful expression. The light in *I Believe* is Christ-light or soul-light; the Sun is Sun of Christ and of my heart.

I Believe could then well be entitled *I Experience*; wherever *believe* and *believed* appear, *experience* and *experienced* could be substituted. I use *believe* and *believed* because it came to me, and I find it has a depth of heart better expressed than *experience* and *experienced*. Experience is everything that lies within the compass of life. Belief, on the other hand, can be of inner sun experiences found only within the human heart in communion with the religious in Man. These qualities suggest *believed* and *believe*, in this particular sense, convey more inward and profound experiences belonging to the heart. The meaning of *believe* is created by the speech sounds of the spoken words of the imagination. This harkens to the fact that thoughts have their origin in spoken words, in spoken language creative of them. In our materialistic age, the vampire of the brain has killing sucked the life out of thoughts by intellectual abstraction, anguish for the artist. Only the spiritual soul's awakening and creative speech can bring the thoughts back to life.

Alan Lindgren
Los Angeles
July 21-22/27, August 4, 2013

xviii

To Rudolf Steiner, to whom I am deeply indebted by my connection to anthroposophy through my good father Arne Lindgren†—my Waldorf education as a child and youth, my travels through Europe and my experiences at the farm Buschberghof and at the Freies Jugendseminar Stuttgart in Germany as a youth and young man, my private studies in anthroposophy since then, and special friendships. Its publishing to key Christian Community pastor-priests who have guided and changed my life by Christ. The stories themselves to the countless storytellers who have, by their art on down the centuries the world over, nourished the souls of and taught the children, inspired the youth, and granted wisdom to adults. My storytelling in this book to Waldorf pedagogy, and to the children, young people, and adults of today and tomorrow who are still able to open their minds, souls, and hearts to the stories with a sense of wonder, love, sorrow or joy, humor, delight, imagination, intuition, discernment, human feeling, and understanding, whereby they can receive what is offered.

Now come to the land of tales and stories, and imagine scenes, events, worlds, exchanges, depictions, and an imagination.
Fill your soul to the brim; become more than a reader as a participant, a friend, and a companion.

First-published

(for Youth and Adults)

Six First-Published Pieces (for Youth and Adults)

> *Anna—A Short Story*
>
> *The Good King and the Wise Princess—A Classic Fairy Tale with a Twist*
>
> *The Forest—Poetic Prose*
>
> *Time—An Elegy*
>
> *I Believe (an Imagination)*
>
> *The Sunset—A Meditation in Prose*

Anna

A pleasant room. Two windows and a door. Four walls, ceiling, and floor. Three chairs, a table small. A bed, and that is all.

It was early morning, and the sunlight was streaming into the bedroom through one of the windows, which was open and faced to the east, across the floor and illumining the upper portion of the bed, which was unmade.

A young woman of twenty years entered the room. She was still in her nightgown, slippers, and cap; and her hair that was long and blonde hung disheveled down over her shoulders and across her bosom.

The lass's eyes were bright blue, her step uneven. She was about five foot four and shapely, if slightly plump. Her nightgown and cap were lavender, her slippers pink.

A maid followed the young woman carrying a tray with breakfast. This consisted in a bowl of hot cereal, a plate with toast smeared with butter and jam, a cup of milk, a glass of apple juice and a small dish with brown sugar. She walked to the chair near the small table that was next to the bed and set the tray on it. Then she placed the bowl, the plate, the cup, the glass, and the small dish on the table. Next she sprinkled the brown sugar onto the hot cereal and poured the cup of milk on top. Returning the small and now-empty dish, and the now-empty cup to the tray, she exited the room.

The young woman got into bed and propped herself up on the pillows. With a spoon that was in the hot cereal that was oatmeal, she stirred it with the brown sugar and the milk. Then she began eating the oatmeal, enjoying the taste of the brown sugar that had melted into the cereal mixed together with the milk. After about three minutes, she bit into the toast and jam that was strawberry, thoughtfully chewing, then took a second bite and did the same. Then she finished eating the toast and returned to the oatmeal, which soon she also finished. Finally, she drank the glass of apple juice, savoring its sweetness.

The empty dishes were arrayed indifferently on the small table, and the young woman looked blankly over to the open window as a sound had reached her ear. It was a sparrow's song, and the little sparrow was perched on the windowsill. She found a few crumbs left from the toast on the plate and put them next to her on the bedspread. The sparrow flew over to her, alighting on the bed and pecked at the crumbs, daintily devouring the tidbits.

The sparrow was not afraid rather trusting, for this ritual was repeated each morning, and it felt happy and at home on the bed next to the young woman, who had just fallen asleep, as she was wont to do after taking her breakfast in bed at this time of day each day. Meantime the sparrow had hopped onto her right hand where a crumb had never left, unlike the others to the bedspread, and it pecked and ate this one too, although the young woman was altogether unaware, wrapped in the folds of pleasant dreams of fattening foods and delicious drinks, and of the smooth silken nightgown that actually caressed the soft skin of her arms and neck.

When she awakened the sparrow had gone, and a little clock that stood on another chair was chiming ten o'clock. In swift but easy movements, she got out of bed and quietly changed from her nightclothes into a dress that was draped over the third chair. The dress was turquoise, and had you seen her eyes they would have appeared green as they were changeable, which I did not tell you earlier. On her feet she now wore emerald green dress shoes, and a string of pearls hung around her neck, their white luster whiter than the pale skin they adorned. Strung between the pearls, very small, were discs of silver that matched her diamond-inlaid silver earrings.

Now she brushed her lovely hair that was abundant as her figure was endowed. In place of her nightcap she put a simple silver band that held her flowing blonde locks of hair from her radiant face, tumbling down her back. She took several of these wondrous locks and strewed them carelessly over her bare shoulders.

Looking at her face in the mirror that she took from a drawer in the small table, she applied pink lipstick to her lips and that was all. In these clothes and with these ornaments she ran out of the room and down the stairs, for it was nearly ten-thirty and a certain gentleman was due to meet her at the front door to the house, and she wanted to rehearse the greeting she had composed for him on the previous evening, to impress him with her manners.

This was unnecessary as the gentleman already understood her perfectly well, her naive childlike demeanor and feminine playfulness, and he trusted her friendliness without question, which he knew was as genuine as it was natural. He welcomed all these things as qualities inherent in the metal she wore in her necklace, earrings, and headband, the fair and precious silver, which mirrors with luster. For she was fair and precious while also young.

Are not lightness and gaiety young? Are not all those of silver old but ever young at heart? Such was Anna, for that was her name. Youthfulness belies the weight and sorrow of their step, the wisdom of these slowpokes. Therefore twofold is the nature of the mirroring Moon, and Anna was Moon's child forever wandering in the night.

This morning, though, the gentleman was her escort to a luncheon at the Laguna Hotel, where she would be pampered as a princess, not suffering as a poor homeless orphan beneath the Moon by the sea.

Yet Anna was an orphan from age seven when her parents had both died in a carriage accident, leaving her with the maid, a dog, and the house by the sea. The dog, a little Pekinese named Pearly, had died when Anna was nineteen, and so her maid Mirabelle, the house, and the sea were all that remained to remind her of her happy childhood.

Anna

She had her food. So much that gave her pleasure had not changed and only added to her voluptuousness, so alluring to the men. When the tall and handsome George discovered Anna sitting alone on the boardwalk at the little Café Alden one afternoon, the gentleman stopped and inquired if he might pay the bill. Would you join me for dessert first? Anna had asked. George was agreeable, and so began their dating, now three weeks in progress. But Anna, unaccustomed to the flattery of a gentleman, always sought to act as a fine lady does, though she was ignorant of what this must be, and so gave attention to her lovely person, making her appear only sweeter and more appealing than she truly was.

George did not mind, though he would have been as pleased had Anna behaved the rather homely orphan of two-thirds her young life such as she was. Only gradually did he coax her hidden grief from her, and only gradually did Anna relax her withdrawn attitude in the presence of knowing George, good fellow that he was, though she retained her secret inborn hidden wisdom.

The luncheon was a lavish affair, and all the couples dressed for the occasion. Anna, in her quiet way, was particularly appealing. Many were the men who glanced her way, and to her delight.

Simplicity best describes this special person, and simple were her charms. Anna's dress and manner only enhanced her loveliness, and George enjoyed his companion more and more with time. Time ages slowly. So with the young beauty seems forever. They seem to dance in dreams of love, as couples on the dance floor to the whirl of music and under the intoxication of wine.

Back in the house with Mirabelle, life was ordinary and routine. This suited Anna, who sought naught else. She only missed her beloved Pearly, so when George called on her one Monday morning carrying a little Cocker Spaniel for her own, Anna was so happy she squealed with unrestrained joy.

She named him Sammy, and soon the two were contented pals. Anna tied ribbons on his head. He only wagged his tail. She clapped her hands. He ran to her with glee. She called his name. He looked up at her with his sad eyes full trusting in his trusting mistress. But mostly they sat quietly together, Anna reading a book and Sammy at her feet.

Mirabelle was a short and stocky thirty-nine year-old widow from France. Her husband had been a petty clerk. Mirabelle left France for England after his death from heavy drinking when she was twenty-one, seeking employment as a maid. After one year working at an inn, Anna's father hired her when she was twenty-two and Anna three.

Mirabelle remained with Anna after her parents died four years later in the accident. Her wages were secured in Anna's will, and she was fond of Anna who required only the loving affection, attention, and care of a faithful servant, which she was. Mirabelle kept the house spotless and was an excellent cook. She did the laundry, which wasn't much, and was thrifty besides. Anna loved her and found in Mirabelle the devotion she had lost with her parents at such a young age. She knew she would never part with her so long they both lived.

George and Mirabelle got along fine. He was gallant as the gentleman he presented, and Mirabelle admired him for his noble qualities and the education she never had. George liked her honesty and work ethic. He was wealthy, she working class. He lived in high society, while Mirabelle associated with the laboring women and men of London's East End.

Beginning December nineteenth it snowed heavily. Frost also appeared on the windows creating their magic patterns. The snowflakes were large and beautiful, softly falling in great numbers. This continued night and day into early morning, Christmas day. When Anna woke up at nine o'clock and opened the window, the sight of the scene blanketed by the snow reminded her of Christmases as a child. Just then Mirabelle called out to her.

Anna

"Anna. It's Christmas morning. Come downstairs to the living room, I've made a fire. We've our Christmas stockings to open, and Master George will be arriving at eleven-thirty. Come, luv."

Anna came running down the stairs, still in her nightgown and slippers. Mirabelle had decorated the room with greens and holly, and mistletoe hung over the entrance. Anna was excited. This was her favorite day in the year.

"Mirabelle. When can we open our Christmas stockings?"

"Let's have our breakfast first, shall we? I've brought rolls with butter and red currant jam, roast beef with cranberry sauce, coffee with cream and sugar, and plum pudding."

"O, Mirabelle. Let's eat. That all sounds delicious."

"Have a seat by the hearth in your father's old chair. I'll serve you promptly."

Anna sat down, and soon the two were enjoying their Christmas breakfast. Sammy was there, too, chewing on a soup bone.

"George wanted me to tell you to dress properly. It's cold, so I've got out your wool coat and boots. The new dress he bought you is hanging on the stairwell."

"Let me see it, Mirabelle."

Anna held up the dress, admiring how nice it would look on her in the mirror. It was lilac with white trim and a low neckline, very becoming. She found a white hat that had belonged to her Mother that matched the dress perfectly.

Sammy barked. He had followed Anna into the hallway.

"Come, Anna. You can dress in a while. Let's have our Christmas stockings."

Now the three were back in the living room. Inside the stockings were fresh oranges imported from Spain, Cadbury® chocolates, and various nuts. Anna found a small wrapped package in hers as well.

"What's in the package, Mirabelle?"

"Open it, Anna. Go on. See what George has bought for you."

"It's from George. It's….it's….a…silver-and-ivory brooch. Imagine how it will look on my new dress. Dear George."

"Give Sammy his doggie treats, Anna luv. He feels left out. I made a Christmas stocking for Sammy too."

"Here little Sammy. Here. Eat your doggie treats."

Sammy ran up to Anna, wagging his tail. Soon he was chomping on some tasty chunks of meaty dog treats.

"What do you think of the Cadbury® with almonds, Anna?"

"Mmm… I'm sampling it right now. It's my favorite chocolate. And the dark chocolate truffle. That's a favorite too."

"Anna. You like all kinds of chocolate, like your dear Mother used to. Let me peel an orange for you. We don't get those much over here in cold England."

"Mirabelle. Tell me about Mother. I remember she was tall."

"Well, Marie was taller than are you, Anna. About one foot six inches, I'd say. She was a real beauty. She had shiny straight black hair and striking grey eyes. She was rosy-cheeked, not pale like yourself, had a nice figure too. Never worked a day in her life. Her parents were wealthy folk. They married her off to a rich gentleman, your father was."

"Wasn't father handsome?"

"Master William was handsome. That he was. Like George, but more serious. He and your Mother were both romantic. They loved one another. I remember the day I came into their employ. They were standing in this very room, hand-in-hand. Said they were going out for a stroll, that they'd be back within the hour to introduce me to the house and my job. Then Master William took Marie by the arm, and outside they went like two young lovers. Very ladylike was your Mother, Anna."

"I remember they were warm. Am I right, Mirabelle? Am I?"

"Yes. Your parents were very warm people. Passionate. But good folk they were, both of them. Honest and kindhearted. Now go and get ready. George will be here in one hour, and you need to shower and dress first."

"I'm going out with George, Sammy. Isn't that cheery, Sammy? With George!"

Sammy wagged his tail. Anna was already upstairs and stripping. Soon you could hear the water running in the shower. A lovely voice was singing, "Good King Wenceslas looked out on the feast of Stephen." Anna was musical and loved to sing in her high clear, soprano voice to feel happy.

When George arrived Anna was standing in the living room, and Mirabelle was pinning the brooch to her new dress. She was beguiling, fair like the shining Moon. George looked dashing in his tuxedo. When he entered the living room, Anna caught him beneath the mistletoe with a kiss. He was taking her to a party at a mansion, then out to a matinee in the afternoon. But the evening was reserved for a cozy restaurant and then his home, for George had a proposition to make.

The party was grand and gay as the show resplendent and well attended. Every one was in good spirits, it being Christmas. The snow made the world a magical place, and small children looked out the windows of their homes, their eyes wide with wonder. Horses pranced in all the streets, pulling carriages. The shops were all closed, the shopkeepers celebrating the holiday with their ken. Many were the flavorful pot roasts and hot stuffed turkeys for Christmas dinner.

After dining on Christmas goose at the Queen's Lodge, an expensive restaurant where George dined on special occasions, he hailed a carriage and rode with Anna to his home on a quiet street.

When they arrived he ushered his date inside, took her coat, helped her remove her boots, and together they sat down on the sofa by the hearth in his study.

George asked Anna if she had enjoyed the day. Why yes, George. It was lovely, really lovely. Then he told her to close her eyes. When she opened them, George was kneeling before her, holding a diamond engagement ring.

"Will you marry me, Anna?"

"George. I'll marry you. You make your Anna so happy."

George slid the ring onto her finger and kissed her hand. The new fiancés slept together by the fire.

The Wedding was set for the third Sunday in April. It was a sunny spring morning, clear if crisp. Mirabelle dressed in a becoming powder blue gown. She was Anna's maid of honor. George was most handsome in black velvet with gold cufflinks.

But Anna was the prize. She wore a snow-white satin Wedding dress with a long train, silver slippers, and a pretty white veil. Afterwards Anna threw her bouquet of cream-white roses and the guests enjoyed Wedding cake. But George went off with Anna in a carriage to the Windsor Inn for their Wedding night. Their bed was King-size, and the room service provided the newlyweds with ample chilled wine and all the privacy couples wish for.

After the honeymoon in the countryside at an estate mansion, George and Anna moved into a large house in a wealthy district of London by the sea.

Mirabelle stayed with Anna as her private nurse. Sammy lived there too until he died at the age of sixteen, which is old for a dog. George enjoyed his life of luxury. And Anna took her breakfast in bed, opening her window every morning to greet a sparrow and feed it crumbs from her toast.

Culver City, California
October 14, 2011
Santa Monica, California
October 17, 2011
Revised Los Angeles
June 30, 2013

The Good King and the Wise Princess

There was a great mountain thirty thousand feet tall and one hundred thousand feet around. A stream flowed from the top down the mountainside and into the broad valley below each spring when the trees sprouted their first green shoots and the first flowers blossomed. Even the sky rejoiced after the long dark cold winter nights, and the little birds sang sweet springtime songs in the trees. Above the regal Sun shone on all God's Creation so that all that was missing was the people.

But they were not missing, because a king, his royal court, castle, and kingdom inhabited the vast mountain land for many miles around. The royal court included ten barons and baronesses, twenty dukes and duchesses, thirty counts, five earls, and three hundred lords and ladies. Ten thousand peasants populated the kingdom. They hunted game deep in the cool forests for the king and his royal court, and sowed and harvested grain in the sundrenched fields as well. But alas, the wealthy king had no queen or children.

Well, one day (it was autumn when a light breeze blew) a messenger came running to the castle posthaste. When he announced himself at the gate, the great but sorrowful ruler granted the messenger audience, but he had been so sad for so long that nothing could lift his heavy spirits any more. He had no queen. When the messenger entered the king's hall where the good man sat on his throne, he was addressed with due courtesy and asked what message he brought. The messenger handed the king a scroll, saying it came from another kingdom far away. The good king thanked the messenger, opened the scroll, and read:

> *I am an old king living alone with my daughter five*
> *great mountains away from your kingdom. I have no*
> *heir to the throne and heard that you have no queen, so*
> *I thought that perhaps you might like to meet my*

daughter as it is possible you might make her your queen. She is twenty-two years old—of marrying age— rich and educated, and loves to play the flute and the harpsichord. Kind to man and child, she is gracious and wise for some one of her tender years, and she would bring you peace and joy. If you are interested, please give me a sign through my messenger, and I will send my daughter to you at once.

The message was signed by the old king himself. Well, at once the good king became hopeful, and he gave the messenger two pure-white turtledoves as a sign to send the young princess to him.

First, however, a long freezing winter arrived. The snow was unusually heavy that year, and travel between mountains was impossible. So the good king waited and waited. There seemed no end to the snow; never in one hundred centuries had it snowed so much. When the Sun finally announced the beginning of spring, and the winter snows melted, and brooks and great rivers flowed, a small party consisting in a princess with long black hair and five ladies-in-waiting began the long journey to the castle of the hopeful king. All manner of little birds and brightly colored butterflies accompanied the travelers, making an otherwise arduous trip light. Big bright billowy white clouds parted, revealing the bluest sky and a resplendent pulsing sun above. It was indeed a most beautiful day when they arrived at the great castle. When the small retinue announced themselves at the gate, the king's servants ran to greet them, and soon the good king invited the princess into the grand hall where he sat on his throne. But when he looked at the young lady, what did he see? The plainest girl—why, she could have been a mere commoner (except for her long raven hair)—stood before him. It seems the young princess read the king's thoughts, because it was she who spoke first:

"Great king, I am a rich and educated princess. I play the flute and the harpsichord. I am kind to man and

child, and I am gracious and wise for a maiden of such tender years—twenty-two, to be exact. With these qualities, I would bring you peace and joy. Further, if you take my hand in marriage and make me your queen, I have reason to believe you will not be disappointed!"

Well, the good king thought about what the wise princess said, and he agreed to marry her. The next day, the castle was decked with finery for the special occasion. Royal red velvet adorned every tabletop, door, wall, and hallway. Sprigs of forest green spruce were placed everywhere, filling the air with their fresh scent, and large white candles lit up the great hall. Expensive porcelain with gold tableware and crystal glasses were set on great wooden tables in the dining room for the Wedding feast. Meanwhile, the royal chefs were hard at work in the kitchens preparing the food for four hundred guests, baking the bread and pastries, roasting the meat and potatoes, frying the vegetables, and decorating the cakes. A priest officiated at the ceremony, where the good king and wise princess were made man and wife.

On the next morning, as he lay comfortably propped up in bed on plush satin pillows in the royal chamber, his new queen stood before a mirror next to the royal bed, while a lady-in-waiting combed her long black hair. Then the king happened to look into the mirror from behind her from where he saw her reflection.

> *"Never has one of the fair sex surpassed you in beauty as you are now while your long black hair is being combed before this mirror!"* he spoke with great astonishment and enthusiasm.

Without the least surprise the wise queen turned to face her new husband and replied:

The Good King and the Wise Princess

> *"My long raven hair shines when it is combed. I told you, you would not be disappointed if you married me. All that was necessary was one night of marriage to a good king to transform my apparent plainness into great beauty. It has not been said for no reason beauty is in the eye of the beholder."*

And that is the story of the good king and the wise princess.

Los Angeles
June 2-4
Revised
June 29-30, 2013

The Forest—Poetic Prose

Deep in the forest the moss shone like emeralds. The toadstools were like castles, the stones like thrones. And there among fallen logs (like sleeping giants), a kingdom of faeries danced and drank wine. They did so quite merry until one bright day, the Sun in her power shone in her great way. The sunlight poured through the trees' branches received and onto the kingdom of faeries believed. The fairies heard unmistakably the Sun's great warm voice, *"Cease now your partying, and hear me rejoice. Christ is a babe and He lies here today. Deep in this forest keep Him safe from harm's way. He is the Saviour of all men and ye. He is the Child of faerie Marie. Gather your instruments and play Him a song. Tend to His Mistress of faerie belong. Tell Christ a story of destiny long. Tell Him of John and His grace will grow strong."*

At once all the faeries did as the Sun spoke. The Child they tended beneath the great oak. And Mary and Jesu protected they sure. The Child grew in strength and in God did endure. The forest became humankind, all the world. And faerie and prophet and king Christ He ruled. Today the kingdom of faeries becomes martyrs like John join salvation's work's Son. The kingdom of kings and queens, rulers becomes teachers and saints of almighty Christ-Sun. And that is the story of faeries, each one. Christ is the Word in the world become.

Los Angeles
June 16
Revised
June 21
June 30, 2013

Time—An Elegy in Prose

The early morning air was foggy with mist. Tombstones, some bare and abandoned, some well-cared for and lovingly decorated with roses of many colors, stood in rows surrounded by recently-mown grass, green and doubly damp with dewdrops. I walked among these tombstones, thoughtful to the dead not found in their remains buried in this old graveyard.

Time erases earthly memory, replacing it with fresh life, much as dead plants, mere corpses of what once germinated, sprouted, grew, budded, and blossomed; wilt to decompose in the sun-warmed wet soil whence new plants birth, live, and grow in the vital air and clear, radiant sunlight. Water is the key to life, fresh water for life as fire to the spirit, human and divine.

Leap then, o Soul of Man, in the great bonfire of midsummer, in the eternal flames of the Sun, earth and heaven garlanded with green ivy of earth of death and color flower of life of heaven. Even as we mourn the gloomy night of spirits, the deceased who come to comfort us in the graveyards of our lives; we rejoice in the good day of the year, Sun of Christ and of our hearts, who gives us His inner measured rhythms for inward feeling and thought sublime, we revere in His warm and clear sun- and soul-light.

Culver City, California
July 13
Revised Los Angeles
July 14
July 18
July 28, 2013

I BELIEVE (an Imagination)

I believed. In my belief I felt feeling. In my feeling I found thinking. In my thinking I beheld light. About the light shadows fell like grey rose petals. The shadows like grey rose petals faded away, revealing a world of color. The world of color bathed my soul in beauty. My soul bathing in the beauty of color smiled tenderly and lovely like little flower-blossoms. My soul smiling tenderly and lovely like little flower-blossoms became windows to the world. The windows to the world opened to allow the sunlight to stream in. The in-streaming sunlight warmed my heart and shone clear through my soul. I felt the warm sunlight on my heart, and I thought the clear sunlight shining through my soul. And I believed again. I believed in feeling. I believed in thinking. I believed in the light that dispels the shadows of darkness like fallen grey rose petals. And the source of the light in which I believe is the Sun. Amen.

Los Angeles
June 20, 2013

The Sunset—A Meditation in Prose

I watched the Sun setting in the west, a witness to this event and a writer of words worthy of Sun-descriptions as deep as drops of dew in a blue bell blossom and as beauteous as a billowy bright white Christ-cloud appearing in a powder blue sky. I wondered where the Sun goes each night after sunset and why She disappears from sight. Is it the other side of reality beyond to dimensions of the world of spirit? Is it to immortality of soul each achieves, we who sleep and die in Christ? Is it because the light requires replenishment from Sun-deeds of yesterday for the coming, new day? The sunset is the initiation of light, Christ's passion and crucifixion, a blessing sacred as a sacristan in human hearts. We see the colors dear; they deepen across the sky. Then, of final light, they fade replaced by colorless grey. Soon the vast night opens her gates of starry pools and another mystery appears, fathomless but seen in a thousand thousand sparkling stars clear in the black sky. Time is a thing past; eternity reigns in stillness, supreme until the dawn of a new day of light, the road on earth the mystery of birth and death. We know the great change, the unborn to birth on earth to immortal divine life to mortal earthly life once more. Reincarnation is the karmic path, our journey to perfection in Christ. Death is the light we see; all else disappears from sight. Only Christ is essence; only He is ours. We know God the All-Father, He who reigns in heavens above.

Los Angeles
July 7
Revised
July 18
July 28, 2013

Republished

Two Fairy Tales for Youth and Adults

The Fairy Tale of the Blue Nightingale and the Little White House Mouse

The Fairy Tale of the Princess and the Stream

The Fairy Tale of the Blue Nightingale and the Little White House Mouse

Once upon a full moon there sang a blue nightingale truly and deeply beneath the starry lights of an August night. She sang her plaintive melody in swooning alto tones echoing across the ravines, through the caves, and over the hills far and wide. Her song came from the soul of the Moon, round and full. No human being who heard her singing this night could go away unchanged, so enchanting was her melodious voice. Indeed, peasant children and young princes and princesses became so enraptured that they were blinded by the haunting beauty of her song, and they stood there entranced, gazing lost at the full white Moon.

When their parents found them on the following morning, they were naturally very concerned, for their children took no interest in their food, their chores, their lessons, or even in the other children. But their parents, farmers, farmers' wives, kings, and queens, did not know why their beautiful children sat and stood staring emptily into space, for they had not been out that fateful August night and heard the enchanting song of the blue nightingale.

The night-blooming cereus, whose blossoms only flower one night of the year, had blossomed that August night of the full white Moon under the same spell of the blue nightingale, huge white blossoms which faded and wilted by sunrise. The beautiful children were also pale white like the blossoms of the night-blooming cereus and like the white Moon, and they took on a ghastly white pallor like the white flowers of this night-blooming plant, fading and wilting in their interest in daily life to the point of a haunting death-like existence.

Reprinted with permission from Alan Lindgren, *The Magic of the Stars* (Culver City: Sun Sings Publications, 2004 and 2005), 192–195; and *Kings & Commoners, Mouse, Magic and More* (2011), 67–72.

The Blue Nightingale and the Little White House Mouse

Unlike these blossoms, which had died, these moon children were still very much alive, only apparently frozen in time and thought as they remained under the spell of the blue nightingale and her full white August moon. They lived under this spell as enchanted children of the night, nor could they sleep any more, small and pale and alone without being able to respond to the warmth and affection of their parents and of the other children, or of the golden summer Sun.

Now there lived in a barn on a farm by the castle a little white house mouse. This mouse was small and curious-looking, with a long soft, white tail, two small white ears pink inside, two small pink eyes, two rows of small white teeth, four small pink paw-hands, and a cute chubby white body.

This little house mouse was born to a long line of royal house mice dating back to the time of Christ. He was born of noble mice parents in AD 1328, and he too was outside on that fateful August night of the full Moon and of the enchanting song of the blue nightingale.

But this little white house mouse was immune to the strange enchantment magic, for he was protected by the warm royal red blood of his lineage dating back to the life of Christ. So although he heard the strange haunting melody of the blue nightingale and saw the full white Moon, and also witnessed the enchantment of the spell over the moonchildren, he remained out of harm's way.

He decided before sunrise to make an antidote from the petals of the night-blooming cereus which, on Michaelmas Eve, on September 28th of the next month, would free the enchanted moonchildren from the spell which bound them.

Our friend, the little white house mouse, went to work right away. He knew the secret of the moonchildren, for like them he too was a moon soul, a moon house mouse, and he carried in his two front pink paw-hands this moon secret of the universe through his hereditary line of royal house mice dating back to the time of Christ 1344 years before.

With his small pink paw-hands he busily set about working to prepare a magic broth made of the petals of the night-blooming cereus that, on Michaelmas Eve, would save the children. He was working very hard drawing sweet spring water from an underground well by the cave to stir with the petals to serve as the antidote.

Meanwhile the farmers, farmers' wives, kings, and queens learned of the affliction of the children of the other class, that both classes were equally devastated by this strange malady. They gathered together, peasants and royalty, each night to discuss what they might do to help their dear children.

Now the farmers knew about our friend, the little white house mouse, for though he never revealed his secret of the Moon, he and his ancestors were known to help estranged children and to cure all manner of ailments, from toothaches and stomach aches, to insanity and brain disorders. This was even recorded in the folk legends of the peasant-farmers, so they implicitly trusted our little friend, even though he never divulged his moon secret of the universe passed on down the centuries through the hereditary line of his ancestors.

One day, as our little friend the white house mouse scurried about the field busying himself as usual, as house mice are wont to do, the farmer who worked this field came upon him and asked him whether something might be done to help the poor moonchildren.

The little mouse only replied, "*On September Twenty-Eight, bring your children, not too late, to the cave beside this well, there their health restored pray tell*." Then our dear little house mouse dashed off in a hurry to tend to his affairs.

Now this farmer, a man of good peasant stock, was known for his mouth because he could not keep a secret, and our mouse knew this perfectly well. That is why he appeared there in the field at this particular time when and where this farmer, famous for his love of speaking, came out to draw some water at the well. For our little mouse-friend knew very well that he would be *the* one to spread the word to all of the other parents.

And this is just what happened.

Five minutes later, the farmer told his wife the rhyme he had learned by heart. She told the other farmers' wives, and all of them told their farmer-husbands, until all of the parents of the enchanted peasant moonchildren knew the rhyme by heart.

The Blue Nightingale and the Little White House Mouse

Next, the king in the neighboring castle received the good much-speaking farmer who brought the rhyme fresh from the little white house mouse, for our farmer-friend knew this king and had politely asked to have an audience with him.

The king, a regal and noble ruler, learned the rhyme himself, and soon he had told the other kings and their queens this rhyme as well. Now they each knew it by heart: *"On September Twenty-Eight, bring your children, not too late, to the cave beside the well, there their health restored pray tell."*

At their next nightly meeting, every farmer, farmer's wife, king, and queen who was either a father or a mother of an enchanted moonchild, began in unison to recite the rhyme aloud. Surprised, they all discovered that everyone else knew this rhyme word-for-word, just as they themselves did, and everyone joyously began to laugh.

Then all at once there was silence, for they all came to the realization together that their children would be healed of their strange illness if they brought them to the cave on Michaelmas Eve, and not too late.

Meanwhile, our good friend the white house mouse was finishing his preparations. Finally, on September 27th, just before midnight, he stirred the petals of the night-blooming cereus into the rapidly boiling sweet well water, thus making the broth that was to be the antidote for the children.

As expected every moonchild was brought to the cave by its parents before nightfall. Just before the sun was about to set in the west, our friend the white house mouse appeared at this cave by the well. He stood up on a table and lifted his voice so that everyone could hear him, saying, *"Thank you for appearing here. The good antidote is near. Bring your children one by one. They will feel the golden Sun."*

Just then, the last golden rays of the setting Sun streamed into the cave and shown upon the faces of the children. And the house mouse sprinkled the antidote onto their eyes, and these beautiful moonchildren were welcomed into the waiting arms of their parents, whose warmth and affection they now returned with many hugs and kisses.

The Blue Nightingale and the Little White House Mouse

The blue nightingale was never heard to sing again. The farmers, their wives, and their peasant children, and the kings, queens, and their princely children all lived happily ever after.

And the little white house mouse? He busies himself between the barn and the field, stopping to chat with the good farmer who so loves to talk.

Culver City
Inglewood, California
August 21, 2004
Revised Los Angeles
June 30, 2013

The Fairy Tale of the Princess and the Stream

Once upon a time there was a stream. The stream flowed down the mountainside, through the forest, down ravines, across valleys, over meadows, and finally, into the sea. The stream carried poppies, daisies, pansies, roses, and daffodils, brought with it all manner of flowers by its flowing, swirling banks.

There was a princess who lived with her ageing father in a great castle atop the mountain. She had no playmates except for the forest-spirits, the flowers, the mosses, the clouds, and the trees. Although it was her eighteenth birthday on this fine September morning, she had never met a young man in all her life.

Her father did occasionally receive visitors from distant lands, but these were all either kings well on in years like him, or also regal and dignified queens accompanied by beautiful young ladies in waiting.

But the princess, Violet Venus by name, was far more beautiful than any of these ladies. Indeed, she was the most beautiful princess ever to have graced the known world. Young Venus could often be seen out in the royal gardens watering the Princess tree, a bush with large violet blossoms and rich green leaves. She lived in a fairy tale dream of youth and innocence, singing songs her Mother Mary had taught her when she was but a small child. Queen Mary had died when Venus was only seven years old, leaving her with her father and the court ladies who served him. Venus's father was King John, and he came from a long line of kings dating back to the third century AD.

On this special morning, September 10, 1274 AD, fair Venus came gracefully running down the mountain from the castle into the great forest called Sepulchre, and she paused when she heard the sound of running water. As she approached its source, all kinds of small birds, such as bluebirds, finches, sparrows, and songbirds; and sprites, sylphs,

Reprinted with permission from Alan Lindgren, *The Magic of the Stars* (Culver City: Sun Sings Publications, 2004 and 2005), 196–202; and *Kings & Commoners, Mouse, Magic and More* (2011), 73–83.

water-nymphs, and undines, came out to greet her. "Good day!" said the princess delighted and delightfully. "Good day!" they all sang and laughed.

Sepulchre was long known in legend to be the place of secret sacred mysteries. It was said that the Holy Grail had passed through this ancient forest in the year 314 AD, and that three drops of the Blood of our Lord and Saviour Jesus the Christ had spilled from the Grail cup into the river Sangre on its journey from the Holy Land. There had been, on rare occasions, eyewitness accounts that Sangre had turned to blood for brief periods since this event in the year of our Lord 314 AD. This is where the rivers got its name, Sangre.

When Venus stepped through an opening in the woods, she entered a meadowed clearing where the stream ran cool and clear. This stream ran into the river Sangre, contributing its waters to its bigger flow on the way to the sea. Venus hopped lightly and easily onto a large flat stone in the middle of the stream, while a small white butterfly alighted on her shoulder.

"Hello, little butterfly," said the princess. "Hello," said the little butterfly, dusting Venus's neck with the silky soft angel-powder from its wings. Fair Violet Venus then knelt down like a fawn, cupping her two hands and dipping them into the water. Just then a storm of rain clouds gathered directly over the meadow and stream and rained three drops of blood into the waters.

At that precise moment, Venus drank the stream's water from her small beautiful cupped hands. As she drank the pure sweet liquid, it changed in an instant into grape juice, turning purple.

"This water tastes just like grape juice!" she exclaimed, without opening her bright blue eyes. As she breathed in and out deeply, the grape juice trickled through her breast, refreshing her heart and lungs from the inside. "This is the best water I have ever tasted," young Violet Venus declared. Slowly, she stood up from her kneeling position. Just then the Sun chased away the rain clouds and shone radiant upon her long golden hair.

When she opened her eyes, Venus felt strangely different than she had ever felt before, taller and more splendid, stronger and lovelier. Her skin and face shone like the Sun, and a swan stopped next to her, bidding Venus to climb on her back.

This Venus did, while six hundred faeries appeared from Sepulchre, dancing and playing on stringed instruments. A bluebird dropped a pomegranate into Venus's open hand. A cardinal gave her a lime in the other hand. Three songbirds flew over her perfect head singing a sweet September tune.

Next, the swan told the princess to eat the pomegranate seeds and drink the juice from the lime, which she did. Her complexion turned rosy on the cheeks, while her hands shone a lustrous light lime green. Assured that Venus was holding onto her neck, the swan spread her wings and flew up into the sky toward the Sun. It was noon exactly, and the clouds were now all big billowy white, emanating bright white Christ-light.

When the swan had flown up as high as the clouds, the Sun began to speak to Venus. She was startled, to say the least, for she had never heard the Sun address her while she rode on the neck of a large white swan before. But the Sun only said, "Do not be startled Princess Venus, for greater things shall you see and hear today before I set in the west."

Now the swan turned and flew westwards, over the mountains and beyond the kingdom of her father King John. Venus saw many great forests and rivers below, and many kingdoms came and went, before the swan began her descent. The princess saw three ships in the distance, golden ships loaded with cargo and with great billowing sails. So she knew they were at the sea, with the ocean glimmering beneath the Sun. It was nearly sunset.

The swan landed on a small, ordinary-looking wooden roof and told Venus she would be spending the night there. Venus was very surprised, for she had always slept in her princess chambers from the time she was born eighteen years before. She asked the swan how she could sleep on a wooden roof outside in the cool night air. The swan replied that she was not allowed to fall asleep, but had to wait until her Saviour came to fetch her at midnight.

"Who is my Saviour?" asked the princess. "It is He Who gave His Life for thee and for all mankind," replied the swan. Just then a breeze blew up. The swan said to Venus, "Fear not, for the Saviour is aboard the third ship, and He is making haste to fetch thee." The swan assured Venus she would be fine until He arrived at midnight and then said to her, "You shall drink grape juice again before He comes to fetch thee." The princess thought, "Surely I have seen and heard many a strange thing this day of the eighteenth anniversary of my birth." The swan explained to her that it was time to part, but gave Venus three of her long white feathers first. Then she spread her wings and, lifting high up into the sky, disappeared in the west.

The princess took a deep breath of the cool sea air. She felt strangely calm, like something wonderful was soon to happen to her. As she turned to make herself more comfortable on the wooden roof, a golden finch flew by and said, "Fair princess, thou art Venus, King John and Queen Mary's daughter. I am here to bid thee a good night. But do not fall asleep, for thou must be awake when the Saviour comes to fetch thee at midnight." When Venus was about to protest that she could adjust to her new outdoor bedroom in order to get some sleep after such a long and strange day, a canon fired in the distance from one of the three ships. Startled, she turned in the direction of the canon and forgot any notion of sleep.

There over the ocean was the most beautiful sunset she had ever seen in her eighteen years on earth. There were thousands of tiny, wispy clouds floating across the sky over the horizon. They were a brilliant peach-blossom color, fanning out to rose and pink. Venus stood up on the wooden roof so that she could better see this wonderful sunset. "Surely this is a magic kingdom," she thought, "for I have never before seen such a castle in the sky." Venus meant the cloud-castle of clouds and color-light in the heavens. And she composed this little poem:

The Magic Kingdom

A magic kingdom in the sky
A magic kingdom up on high
I saw it golden in the clouds

Shining in bright radiant shrouds.

A magic castle up above
A magic mountain of pure love
I saw it in the heavens grand
A heavenly magic mountain-land.

A magic castle smiling there
In the golden glowing air
A magic mountain mystery
Up in the heavens for to see

A magic kingdom where dwell them
Little elfin faerie men
A magic kingdom there of light
In the heavenly landscape bright.

A magic castle in the air
Built of clouds all faerie-fair
Made of airy, radiant light
On a magic mountain bright.

A magic castle robed in sun
On a magic mountain won
By enchantment 'fore the night's
Starry merry mystic lights.

Now the Sun has set in love
Now the faeries dance above
Join the heavenly mystery
Dwell the night most magically.

But remember sunset's love
But recall the clouds above
The magic kingdom in the air

The Princess and the Stream

The magic kingdom radiant fair.

Next, she noticed how the colors had changed to orange-golden and a red to the sides, before the Sun finally set in the sea. She felt strangely contented and rested, yet longed to fall asleep and dream of many things, but she remembered what the swan and the goldfinch had both said, and resolved to stay awake until midnight. She held the three soft white feathers lightly in her long, white fingers, wondering where her friend the swan was now.

Now storm clouds had gathered over the ocean and were swiftly moving over land. Within minutes, the rains were pouring down, drenching the young princess, who was wearing but a simple white gown. Ordinarily, Venus would have been shocked to think she was caught in her thin gown on a wooden roof in the pouring rain by the sea at night, but after the events of the preceding day, it would take more than this to surprise her, and she actually felt greatly relieved and refreshed by the sensation of the cooling rain pouring across her young body. The princess cupped her hands to catch some of the rain in order to drink, because she was thirsty, and as she drank, three drops of the Blood of Jesus Christ rained into her cupped hands, changing the rain into purple grape juice.

"This rain tastes just like grape juice," Venus thought. "How delicious it is!" But as it was nighttime and dark, she could not see that it actually was grape juice she was drinking. As the grape juice trickled through her breast, she breathed in and out deeply, filled with joy and refreshed from within. As she stood there in the pouring rain, the princess seemed to grow several inches taller, and her wet head and body shone silver in the moonlight.

Little by little, the rain came down more slowly, from pouring down in sheets to coming down in big large drops, to tapping lightly and making a lovely sound on the window panes of the buildings surrounding the barn where Venus was perched in her silver glory. Her white gown, now soaked through and through, was see-through, so that had anyone seen her she was as good as nude, but as there wasn't a soul around, she was only nude before the full round white Moon.

Finally, the rain stopped altogether. A warm summer breeze filled the night air, caressing the princess's body, drying off her white gown. Her lips were full and red, her cheeks all rosy sweet, her bosom swelled soft and warm, and her hips were round and sensuous. But her romance was not of the ordinary kind, for in her maidenly innocence, she awaited only the coming of the Lord and Saviour of mankind. She would be His bride and He her bridegroom.

Venus breathed the night air and noticed how all had become still. Everything was perfectly clear after the rainstorm, and thousands of stars shone sparkling in the night sky. She could see Saturn and Jupiter, Mars and Venus, Mercury and, of course, the full Moon. And the Romance of Venus filled the entire sky, and with the sky the breast of fair Venus, eighteen-year-old princess, daughter of King John and Queen Mary.

By and by the hours before midnight passed in a dream of stars, and Christ Jesus had long since stolen from His ship onto the land, making His way toward the barn. At midnight all of the church bells in the town began to chime loudly. Venus looked up, still standing atop the wooden roof. Christ Jesus climbed the roof of the barn and looked quietly at the princess without saying a single word. A breeze picked up and took a lock of her blonde hair, blowing it across her beautiful face. She turned and saw Him standing there, dressed in shining golden armor, a crown of gold and diamonds on His Head.

"I have come to fetch thee," He spake gently, offering her His strong and gentle Hand. Venus smiled tenderly and put her hand in His. The wooden barn transformed into a great Church Cathedral, and Christ Jesus and Princess Violet Venus were joined in Holy Matrimony before the Altar of God by the Holy Spirit, and the Congregation was the Heavenly Hosts singing Songs of Praise, and King John was there too, and all of the other kings and queens, and Queen Mary had come in spirit along with St. Francis of Assisi and the other saints, St. Paul, St. Matthew, St. Mark, St. Luke, St. John, St. Stephen. Mother Mary was there, and Mary Magdalene, and all of the saints were there. And the Sun shone so brightly that the Cathedral was as day, and there was much celebration and joyful music making.

The Princess and the Stream

Then the kings and queens exited the Church, filling the streets in one stream of humanity singing songs together, and the Cathedral changed into a mythical horse with wings, a Pegasus, and flew up with all the saints and the dead, and with the heavenly hosts, and Christ Jesus lifted His young Bride Princess Venus up into His strong and gentle arms, and a great golden Horse galloped to His Side. The Saviour put the Princess on the golden Horse, telling her to hold onto its Mane, and He jumped behind her taking the Reins.

And the Horse *was* Pegasus, and together the new Bride and Bridegroom rode up to the Sun and to Venus, with Apollo riding his sun-chariot and Aphrodite preparing their Bedchamber. And there was a long and glorious Wedding Night. And *that* is my story.

Inglewood, California
September 10, 2004
Revised Los Angeles
June 30, 2013

Five Folk Tales for All Ages

The Folk Tale of the Baking Potato Farmer

The Folk Tale of the Two Tom-Tom Bird Cousins

The Folk Tale of the Green Swedish Leprechaun

The Folk Tale of the Little Spanish Cobbler

The Folk Tale of Frederick and the Village of Fortune

The Folk Tale of the Baking Potato Farmer

There once was a very poor farmer who grew only potatoes. These were a special kind of potatoes. They were baking potatoes. This poor farmer never sold his potatoes to anyone. But no other farmers in the entire region grew baking potatoes, because they could not for the life of them discover the proper method to do so. They had tried and tried, for many years they had tried. They had tried everything, but whatever they did, they could not grow a baking potato. They did not know if the secret lay in the soil somewhere, or if it had to do with the amount of rain, or in some other aspect involving the climate. But although they tried everything they could think of, they were never able to grow a baking potato. And the farmer who grew only baking potatoes knew this.

So why, you may wish to know, didn't the farmer sell his baking potatoes? After all, he could have gotten the highest prices for them, because they were like precious gold to people for millions of cartwheel circumferences around. Nonetheless, our farmer simply would not sell a single one of his baking potatoes, even though they were in such great demand—as great demand as the Sun is great—in this entire region.

Now it did happen (though only once in a blue moon) that a person or family once or twice in a lifetime—if they were so fortunate—actually had the great pleasure of eating a baking potato. And how, you may wish to know, was this possible, seeing as the only farmer who grew baking potatoes *never* sold them, *never ever*, and not to *any*one, and *not even once*. So I'll tell you. I'll tell you the story, and I'll even give you examples of how—very rarely—some one had the exquisite pleasure to dine on a big fat baking potato. Now listen to my story of the baking potato farmer. Then you'll be in on the secret, too.

Reprinted with permission from Alan Lindgren. *Kings & Commoners, Mouse, Magic and More* (Culver City: Sun Sings Publications, 2011), 91–108.

The Baking Potato Farmer

Each morning at dawn, our poor little farmer would get up, eat a small breakfast of hash-browned baking potatoes (and maybe a fried egg and buttered toast to go with it, if he was lucky on the previous day), together with a small mug of freshly brewed hot coffee (this was the only luxury he ever allowed himself), and load up his little horse-drawn cart with a few dozen baking potatoes. Then he would set out and travel—sometimes quite far—with his little horse-drawn cart loaded with the potatoes. Then, when he came upon a farm, a village, or a town, he would look for the person who had what it was that he needed.

Now as the farmer was very poor, he could never have afforded to buy anything. Indeed he was as poor when it came to money matters, to business matters, and to commerce in general, as he was a farmer. He had no business savvy. He had no business sense whatsoever, and this was why he was and remained so poor.

But he did possess one very valuable piece of wisdom. And this was that because he was the one and only farmer far and wide who knew the secret of how to grow baking potatoes, and because he *never* sold one of his baking potatoes to *any*one, *not even once*, he could very often trade one of his wonderful potatoes for just about anything he needed.

Now it never occurred to him that he could use this prized piece of wisdom to obtain things he did *not* need, things such as diamond-encrusted Swiss-made timepieces; gold-inlaid porcelain plates, saucers and teacups; crystal wineglasses and costly silverware; fine cloth and expensive linen and lace; or imported hard-to-find items like rare spices, silk, satin, and whatnot.

Such thoughts were far from his head, for he was a simple soul who was satisfied with his humble life as a potato farmer, although it is true he sometimes thought to himself (with a certain solemn dignity and peasant pride), he *was* a baking potato farmer and not just any old potato farmer. You see, our potato farmer worked hard. That is how he led a healthy life out in the country where he had become famous for his big baking potatoes.

One fine summer day, George (for that was our poor little baking potato farmer's name) was out looking for some good white corn, for he really *loved* to eat the sweet white corn and had not tasted any in quite some time. So he went in search of a corn farmer, a farmer who grew some really good white corn.

When he came upon a great cornfield, George saw a fancy house standing there like a silver crown, so he went up to the front door, that was fancily decorated with rococo white lace and rich imported green satin, to inquire within, and he knocked.

The corn farmer's wife, who was occupied with her housekeeping chores, opened the door and asked him what was so pressing that he interrupted her important household duties. Our simple potato farmer politely asked whether they had a spare ear or two of white corn. When she said, "Yes we do; as-a-matter-of-fact my husband specializes in growing the finest white corn found anywhere," George grew very excited. But when he offered her one of his baking potatoes in exchange for an ear or two of the corn, she looked at him indignantly and said, "Who do you take us to be? *We* accept only money for our excellent, top-of-the-line corn, check or credit card. After all, we have bills to pay, and a fine pretty house to decorate at that!"

At that she shut the door and strutted off to finish her household duties before her husband returned from the cornfields for dinner, which she had stewing and baking in the kitchen.

When her husband arrived, promptly at 1:00pm to eat his meal of stewed white corn and baked white corn, the housewife exclaimed, "You would not believe what just happened! Some measly baking potato farmer was just here, trying to exchange one of his baking potatoes for some of our excellent corn!" "What did you do?" replied the corn farmer. "Well, of course, I sent him away empty-handed. What kind of a joke was he playing anyway! We have bills to pay, and a house to decorate!"

With that the corn farmer scolded his wife away, saying, "Foolish woman! That poor baking potato farmer is the only farmer who grows those priceless baking potatoes! What a rare pleasure it would have been to enjoy one: —and for only a few ears of our common corn!"

Meanwhile our potato farmer had already moved on in search of a few ears of sugar-sweet white corn. He could already picture himself sitting at his humble wooden table with a wooden plate before him enjoying a warm supper of baked potatoes and corn.

About a thousand cartwheel circumferences down the road, George saw another cornfield, with the tall corn blowing in the breeze and brazen in the golden sunshine. He paused for a moment from his travels to enjoy the fine view, for he could not recall ever having seen such a beautiful cornfield.

Now it so happened this corn really *was* the best corn that could be found in the entire region, and the corn farmer was a tall and goodly man who lived a simple life with his dear wife and their four small children. When our potato farmer came up to the door of this family's home, he paused again. Perhaps here he would find what he had been dreaming of, an ear or two of delicious white corn.

When George knocked, the wife answered the door with a gracious smile on her rosy-cheeked face. "May I help you, good sir?" she asked. "Well," said our potato farmer, "I was hoping you might exchange an ear or two of your tasty white corn for one of my baking potatoes." Immediately the woman called out to her husband, the corn farmer, and their four small children, "Family, come; come quickly! The farmer who grows baking potatoes is here, and he wants to exchange one of his baking potatoes for a few ears of our plain corn!"

Soon the entire family was standing there. The children were looking wide-eyed with wonder at our potato farmer, while the tall corn farmer offered him his big strong warm hand, saying, "Good potato farmer, we have long heard of your fine baking potatoes and have dreamt of having one with our supper. Here, take as many ears of my corn as you please. I do not grow enough in all of my fields to pay you what this is worth."

"Well," said George, "surely I have found in you and your family the kindest of people. I am honored by your offer. Here, take six of my baking potatoes, one for each of you." At that the corn farmer beamed, "Now, my good man. This is too much. Out of the goodness of your heart, you are blessing me and my family with no fewer than *six* of your baking potatoes. Now I insist. Take sixteen ears of my white corn. This is the very least I can do." So George had no choice but to accept. But he insisted on giving the corn farmer and his family sixteen of his baking potatoes.

The two men exchanged their goods, shook hands once more, and returned, each to his own business. As he walked away, George thought to himself, "My, what good fortune I have had," and he pictured himself that evening feasting on sixteen ears of the finest corn in the entire region—and white corn at that. But then his good common sense returned to him, and he thought better. "I'll enjoy four ears this evening, four at supper tomorrow, four on the following evening, and the other four the next."

That is precisely what he did. But he still had many of his baking potatoes in his horse-drawn cart, so he traveled on a ways looking for some fresh butter to have with his corn and baked potatoes, for he had run out of butter the previous day.

Soon he came to a farm where there was a large shiny tin barn. George saw many cows outside grazing. He thought to himself, "Maybe I'll find a farmer here who will exchange one or two horseshoe weights of butter for one of my baking potatoes." So he went inside the barn and found a poor young man who was milking a cow. "Hello," said George, "Do you know where the dairy farmer of this fine place is, for I would like to exchange one of my baking potatoes for some of his butter?" The man scurried off in a hurry, saying, "I'll go to ask him!"

When the young man returned with the dairy farmer, the dairy farmer looked George up and down as though he were a curiosity from the circus. "And *who*, might I ask, do *you* think you are, asking for some of my fine butter in exchange for a baking potato?!" When George replied he was an upstanding baking potato farmer from over yonder, the dairy farmer laughed, saying, "You'll never find such a fool who would give you butter in exchange for a common potato. Nowadays all the dairy farmers accept only money, check or credit card, for we have big bills to pay and large shiny tin barns to maintain." And with that he turned and walked away.

The Baking Potato Farmer

But the young man knew about the baking potato farmer and his wonderful baking potatoes, and he thought to himself what a shame his boss had treated this kind farmer so rudely, passing on such a golden opportunity. He himself had long cherished the hope he and his family would one day feast on a baking potato.

When George saw the man standing there looking so sadly he wanted to cheer him up, so he gave him a big baking potato, saying, "Please, take this and enjoy it with your supper tonight." The man's face lit up at once, and he beamed, "My wife and child will be so proud I met the famous baking potato farmer and that he gave me one of his baking potatoes!" When he learned that the poor young man had a family, George handed him five more of his potatoes, smiled, wished him well, and returned to his travels.

So the little baking potato farmer continued with his search for some butter to enjoy with his corn and baking potatoes. Soon he came to a simple wooden barn where a few happy cows stood outside chewing their cud and swishing their tails on this lazy summer afternoon. The flies buzzed about, and young children were out running and playing tag and hide-and-go-seek.

George stood there for a moment before he called out, "Do any of you know where the dairy farmer is?" A cocky little boy ran up to him and tried to say in a mature voice, "He's my Papa. I'll go and bring him." Our potato farmer took a liking to this spunky little boy, recalling how he had been somewhat like him when he was the boy's age, so he said, "Well thanks, little boy. You won't be sorry for being such a good and helpful child." The little boy was surprised and didn't know what to think. He wondered what good fortune was soon to befall him as he went out in search of his father, the dairy farmer.

When he returned, the boy proudly presented his father, saying, "This is my Papa!" The dairy farmer, a short stocky man, well tanned from the summer sun, introduced himself with the words, "My son really likes you. He said something about his good luck, but I couldn't figure out what he was taking about."

"Well," replied George, "I don't know anything about good luck. To tell you the truth, I came here to see if you would be willing to exchange one or two horseshoe weights of your fine butter for one of my baking potatoes." Now although he didn't know it, this dairy farmer was known for his butter. It was said to be the best butter in the entire region, so sweet it was.

Then the stocky dairy farmer replied, "Are you the baking potato farmer we've heard so much about?" When he said, "Well yes, I guess I must be, because I am the only baking potato farmer in the entire region," the dairy farmer, overcome with joy, nearly shouted to his kids, "Children, this is the famous baking potato farmer every one is talking about!"

Then he turned to his son and said, "Now I know what you meant when you said you were in good luck, little Peter," for this was the cocky little boy's name. Then the dairy farmer said to George, "One of your baking potatoes is worth my butter from two entire months. Here, take twenty horseshoe weights."

"Now," said our little baking potato farmer, "You really are too generous. Because of your generosity, and good little Peter's helpfulness," he added, looking at Peter with a kind smile, "you must take twenty of my baking potatoes." These were the last potatoes in his cart. The dairy farmer was flabbergasted. He was so thankful to the potato farmer, so surprised at his good luck, and so proud of his little son Peter, that he could hardly contain his feelings, and a few tears welled up in his good eyes. He put his arm around his little boy and smiled, for he could not recall a happier day in his whole life. It warmed George's heart to see this good dairy farmer and his son.

Then the potatoes and the butter were exchanged, and the two men parted after a good handshake, agreeing they should do this again sometime when the potato farmer was in the area. As he was leaving with his horse-drawn cart, now empty of baking potatoes, and full with sixteen ears of the finest white corn and twenty horseshoe weights of the sweetest butter in the entire region, George called out to the little boy, "Peter! Thanks again for being such a good and helpful child." With that he set out for his potato farm, eager to cook four ears of the special white corn and bake one of his big baking potatoes to enjoy with that sweet butter.

The Baking Potato Farmer

(There are two different endings to this folk tale, the original ending°
here, and an alternative ending [a] , below.)

° Now there was a neat and tidy little lady who lived on the property
next door to George and his baking potato fields. The two of them
greeted one another from time to time, and George paid her a visit
occasionally. They had grown fond of one another, but neither thought
of pursuing their little friendship beyond their acquaintance. But when
George came around the bend in the road leading up to his home, he
inevitably had to pass by the little lady's house, which was always so
neat and tidy.

On this day, as he had returned early from his bountiful bartering,
George thought that perhaps he might share some of the tasty white
corn and sweet fresh butter with her, even though he knew she ate only
peas and carrots.

So he went up to the door of her little house, that always looked so
inviting because she swept the threshold clean with her little broom,
and then placed her little straw mat before the entrance, to see if she
were home. But when the poor little farmer knocked on the door, he
didn't hear a sound, because the little lady was out in the backyard
washing her laundry on her washing board, for she always did her
laundry every Wednesday (which happened to be this day of especially
bountiful trading), so she didn't hear his knocking. So the little farmer
knocked a little harder, hoping she would be at home to take some of
his corn and butter, but he heard not a sound.

"Really," thought our baking potato farmer, "surely this is unusual!
Martha is *always* at home at three-thirty in the afternoon on
Wednesdays." He could well say this, because Martha (for this was the
neat and tidy little lady's name) had told him as much. So he knocked
much, much harder, certain she would hear him this time, unless she
had suddenly gone hard of hearing, which he didn't believe for a
minute.

Meanwhile Martha had finished washing and rinsing her sheets on
the washing board, and had just hung them neatly and tidily on her little
clothesline to dry, when she remembered she had left her wooden shoes

by the front door of her little house to dry in the sun that morning, because she had rinsed them off to make them spic and span, in case her neighbor George should stop by to visit. She didn't know herself why she had done this, make her wooden clogs spic and span for George, that is, because it had never occurred to her to do something like this before. Nonetheless, there were her clean and dry wooden clogs sitting there by the door waiting for her to put them on. When Martha had come around the corner and was walking toward the front door, she didn't see George standing there, because she was busy thinking about how she looked, and whether she looked neat and tidy.

Now George was facing away from Martha, looking in the other direction. He didn't know what he should do. He couldn't imagine where Martha was, and he certainly could not have guessed she was headed right for him, until she bumped into him, that is!

Now neither of them knew what to say or what to do with himself. This was an awkward moment—the most awkward moment in both of their entire little lives. Martha blushed, and it was she who broke the silence, because she could never hide her feelings from someone—not even as a little girl.

"George! Good gosh! Now look what you've gone and made me say! Here I was just coming to put on my newly cleaned wooden shoes for you, and there you are, standing around—and right in my way!" And she then began to weep copiously, trying to hide her tears of joy and embarrassment.

Now George may have been a simple man, a poor, hardworking baking potato farmer, but he could see that dear Martha was feeling so confused, glad, and ashamed at the same time, so to comfort her and give her his humble support, he patted her gently on the shoulder, saying, "There, there, little Martha, you needn't cry. Here, take my handkerchief and wipe your little nose."

Now Martha was so touched by George's kind gesture that she didn't tell him he had dirtied her blouse (which she had put on just for him) when he patted her gently on the shoulder, and she also knew that if she refused his dirty kerchief she would be hurting his feelings. So she replied, "O dear, dear George. You are too kind. Surely there isn't such a gentleman in this entire region," and at once she forgot all about her embarrassment. Then Martha took the dirty little handkerchief and lightly blew her pretty little nose, for she was a neat and tidy little lady, after all. And then George asked Martha if she would put on her spic and span wooden shoes, because he remembered she had cleaned them just for him, which made him feel very special. Never in his entire little life had a lady sought to please him so. Dear, dear Martha!

It was then that George realized he had always loved Martha, ever since they had first met and visited, because she was always inviting him into her house to wash up (which he never did), because he was such a fine gentleman. And Martha had long felt a tenderness for kind George, because he was always so thoughtful of and gentle with her, and because he always asked her if she would please take some of the produce—in addition to the peas and carrots he brought her regularly—and other foods he brought back with him from his travels with his horse-drawn cart (which she never did because she ate only peas and carrots).

I won't tell you all that happened next, but I *will* tell you the happy ending of a story of how a poor little potato farmer named George, famous for his big baking potatoes, and a neat and tidy little lady named Martha, who never could hide her feelings (not even as a little girl), joined hands in marriage, and raised three children.

One, the eldest, was a boy they named Michael. The two younger children were both girls, and they were given the names Laura and Anne. And the little family never wanted for baking potatoes, as much as their hearts desired. And they never wanted for carrots, peas, corn, or any other vegetables; or for milk or cheese, butter or eggs, bread or meat; or for apples, pears, cucumbers, lettuce, or any other produce, because George went out every morning and traded some of his wonderful baking potatoes for whatever they needed.

And little Martha, who kept their small house neat and tidy, and who always put out fresh clean clothes for George and the children each morning to begin the new day, learned to prepare and enjoy all *kinds* of foods, because her husband insisted she try them. And little George learned to wash his hands and put on a freshly starched shirt—

at least before sitting at the dining table on Sundays at one o'clock in the afternoon, because his wife insisted the finest gentleman in the entire region should always be neat and tidy before sitting down to eat Sunday dinner with his family.

alternative ending [a]

[a] Now it so happened there was an ancient oak tree growing by the road that George always had to pass by on his way back to his baking potato farm and humble abode. On this beautiful summer afternoon, as he had finished with his bartering adventures early, George thought he might take a short nap in the shade beneath this great old oak before returning to his home nearby to unload his white corn and sweet butter. So when he arrived at the foot of the oak he stopped, telling his faithful old horse Tarny (for that was the name of his faithful old horse) to stay and wait for him while he rested up a bit. Then George found a nice even spot in the shade, lay down, and soon fell sound asleep.

Now there lived a gay and greedy tiny elf inside this ancient oak who relished white corn with sweet butter, because it reminded him of his deceased old Mother Mordie, an infamous and wise elf-queen who used to prepare it for him when he was young, and whom he still called on sometimes when casting spells with his little magic wand. When George had fallen fast asleep, this little elf decided to take a look under the tarp that George always draped over whatever he carried in his little horse-drawn cart, because he was also a very curious tiny elf, just as he was always up to no good. So Nicky (for this was the elf's name) quietly stepped out of his oak tree and tiptoed over to the cart, whispering into Tarny's ear to be still.

Tarny asked Nicky why he should be quiet, because he was, after all, a faithful old horse who always looked out for his good master George. But this response perturbed the little elf, who had expected Tarny to comply with his wish without question, so he cast a spell over the old horse to make him be still against his will.

So Tarny had no choice in the matter, and stood there patiently watching while Nicky crept around to the cart, climbed up, and lifted the tarp. When he saw the sixteen ears of beautiful shining white corn and the twenty horseshoe weights of sweet butter, Nicky was so glad that he danced gaily about in little circles, clapping his little hands in delight, and took his magic wand from the empty air.

Now George had always been a sound sleeper, but on this occasion he had accidentally lain down directly on top of a small, misshapen stone, so he was now going in and out of deep sleep, now falling contentedly into dreamland and beyond, now rising up from beyond into unpleasant dreams caused by the small, rough stone under his back.

Well, when Nicky began to dance in little circles and clap his little hands with glee, George woke up, but at once he thought to himself who that might be making all manner of that merrymaking. So he decided he'd best feign sleeping on and watch what was happening with his eyes half-closed. There was the tiny little elf, rubbing his small hands jealously around his little magic wand, eager to steal the corn and butter from the cart, but not wanting to wake up George, who was already awake, so as to avoid any problems.

Right away George realized what was going on, and he set about making a plan to catch the elf and see that justice was done. When Nicky began to sing his wish in an elfin song that was really a charm, singing in a quiet voice, "Corn of the fields all white, butter sweet and light, make your way out of sight!" George noticed that Nicky was rubbing his greedy little hands together around a magic wand as the corn and butter disappeared. So he thoughtfully finished making his plan and started implementing it at once, and this is what George did.

Our little baking potato farmer began to yawn in a very loud voice. As though he were speaking in his dreams, George said, "He who steals my corn; he will be forlorn. He who steals my butter; he will forget his Mother!"

When Nicky heard George's words, coming as though from a dream-state, he became very frightened, because he believed George was a leprechaun, which he was not, and that he therefore knew the infamous elf-queen Mordie was his Mother, which he did not. But tiny Nicky did not know that George was nothing more than a poor baking potato farmer, and nothing less, so he quickly began singing an altogether different elfin song.

"White corn return with butter; instructions take from Mother. Corn of white become gold, pure as the Sun. Butter sweet as dew, gold now turn anew." Then he stopped to see what George would do next. When our little potato farmer yawned again, he called out to his horse Tarny, "Tarny, my horse, see, what my bounty be!"

When Nicky heard George addressing his horse, he grew even more afraid, because he had cast the spell over Tarny to make him stand still, so he sang yet another elfin song that went like this, "Horse once old now turn, young as a green fern; now wake up and stir master your, for sure!" And at that Tarny became ten years younger and walked up to George nudging him.

Now when all of this had happened, George decided to have some more fun with this naughty little elf, so he feigned waking up and, sitting up, called out, "Tarny, Tarny, where is my magic wand? I left it somewhere in this old oak tree the other day, but can't for the summer's day remember where I put it again."

Then tiny Nicky exclaimed, "Wise leprechaun, please, do me no harm! I meant only to dine on some of your white corn and sweet butter like Mommy Mordie used to make! Here, take my magic wand, only do me no harm." And with that the elf handed George his wand, looking up at him with pleading eyes.

Now George was in an altogether different position. He stood up and turned to Tarny, and when he saw his dear old horse younger by ten years, George asked the little elf what had happened. "Well," Nicky replied, "I had cast a spell to make your horse be still so I could borrow some of your corn and butter without disturbing you. But when I learned you are a wise leprechaun, I didn't want you to hurt me, so I cast a little spell over him to make him ten years younger to please you."

"Oh," said George, "so you had yourself in mind when you cast your little magic spell, did you?" With that he returned old Tarny to his rightful age, saying, "You were really up to no good, that is plain. What is your name, little elf?"

"Nicky," said the tiny elf, "at your service." Next, George turned to his little cart, and he saw his sixteen ears of white corn turned into pure gold, likewise his twenty horseshoe weights of sweet butter. Of course he knew what had happened, because he had heard the elf casting the spell, but he pretended he did not and said, "Now, Nicky. Why are my sixteen ears of white corn and twenty horseshoe weights of sweet butter turned to pure gold?"

"Good leprechaun, I feared you would do me harm when you found out I had stolen your bounty, so I quickly cast a little spell over your corn and butter to please you!" At that the elf stepped back fearfully, awaiting the potato farmer's response. "So," George retorted, "again you had your own welfare in mind when you did your little magic trick," and he changed the gold back into white corn and sweet butter.

Now George's plan had run its full course, but still he had to deal with this little trickster, so he said, "Nicky, Nicky, Nicky. Your name be changed to Mickey. Lose your magic powers. Oak tree change to flowers." And at that moment Nicky's name changed to Mickey forever, he lost his magical elfin abilities, and where the great ancient oak had stood for many a decade, summer flowers now grew.

Then the elf said, "O wise leprechaun! I thank ye for sparing me and doing me no harm. But where shall I live now that my house, the great oak, is turned to flowers?" So George waved the magic wand, saying, "Make a tiny house fit for a small mouse. There may Mickey live, harmless toil, and give." And from that moment on little Mickey, the powerless elf, had to work away in his tiny house and give away everything he made.

Finally, George wanted to make sure the tiny elf would not be able to contact the infamous deceased elf-queen Mordie, whom he now knew was none other than Mickey's Mother. So he spoke one final magic spell that went like this, "Mordie, Mordie, Mordie, like a speedy birdie; fly away from Mickey; desert him in a quickie!"

Then George made the magic wand disappear, because he wanted nothing to do with magic, and went back to his baking potato fields and home. That evening, after harvesting a few dozen of his prized potatoes for the coming day's work, he enjoyed one of his fat baking potatoes and four ears of the most delicious white corn with the sweetest butter in the entire region.

Los Angeles
February 24-25, 2007
[a] alternative ending
March 15-16, 2007

The Folk Tale of the
Two Tom-Tom Bird Cousins

There once was a Tom-Tom Bird so rare, o so rare. The Tom-Tom Bird, who lived in Europe, was so rare that he only had one cousin who was also a Tom-Tom Bird. She lived in far away Asia. But as they lived so far away from one another, the two Tom-Tom Birds had never met, each the other.

The Tom-Tom Bird who lived in Europe was named Catchy, because he sang a catchy tune which other birds, like the mockingbird, tried to imitate, but without success. The catchy birdcall that Catchy the Tom-Tom Bird sang went like this: *Hooeeya hey! Hooeeya hey! Hooeeya volley, hooeeya ney!* And then Catchy the Tom-Tom Bird would laugh because he thought how catchy and funny his birdcall sounded.

The Tom-Tom Bird who lived in far away Asia was named Matchy, because all the other Asian birds tried to match her song, though unsuccessfully. *Hooeeya hey! Hooeeya hey! Hooeeya volley, hooeeya ney!* she sang like Catchy. But Catchy did not know that his cousin's name was Matchy as they had never met.

One fine spring day all the different birds of the European continent gathered together in an old forest called the Black Forest that is in Swabia, Germany for a singing contest. Catchy showed up to sing his catchy birdcall to see if he could win the much-coveted prize, which was a trip to China on *The Asia Wind Express.*

Each bird singing in the contest represented a different European country. Because Catchy was the only Tom-Tom Bird in all Europe, he was chosen to represent his own country and kind of bird.

Reprinted by permission from Alan Lindgren, *Michael and Los Angeles* (Culver City: Sun Sings Publications, 2008), 164–169; and *Kings & Commoners, Mouse, Magic and More* (2011), 116–120.

The Two Tom-Tom Bird Cousins

Some of the other kinds of birds represented included the *Fancy Golden-throated French Marseille Bird*, the *Double Dirndl-dancing German Green-bellied Bavarian Blackbird*, the *Yodeling Swiss Eye-ogling Alpine Ostrich*, the *Ostentatious Operatic Italian Bravado Tenor Tufted Titmouse*, the *Red-tailed Spanish High-hopping Hoola Hoop Bird*, the *Yellow-tipped Portuguese Satin-seated Sonnet Bird*, the *Darling Dutch Windmill Bluebonnet Bird*, and the *Dapper Danish Dreaming Do Little Bird*.

Then there were the *Orange-breasted Russian Rolling River Bird*, the *Multicolored Czech Castle Courting Chickadee*, the *Miniature Moldavian Maroon Mockingbird*, the *Lilting Long-tailed Latvian Lavender Lovebird*, the *Lean Light-footed Lithuanian Listening Ladybird*, the *Green-crested Greek Gymnastic Giant Island Bird*, and the *Ukulele Ukrainian Scarlet Whistling Window Tanager*.

Others included the *Nocturnal Norwegian Northern Nightingale*, the *Sonorous Swedish Sweet-singing Songbird*, the *Elegant Estonian Evergreen Easter Bird*, the *Red-bellied Romanian Royal Beige Bird*, the *Merry Macedonian Melodic Mistletoe Bird*, the *Beautiful Black Bulgarian Schoolboy Bird*, the *Artful Antics Albanian Acting Bird*, the *Sun-worshipping Serbian Swallow-tailed Sunset Swan*, and the *Slow Slovenly Slovakian Silver-sleeved Stork*.

Still others were the *Bright Long-feathered Belgian Borage Blue Jay*, the *Legendary Lovely Finnish Glistening Lake Bird*, the *Little Lapp Rust-colored Reindeer Redpoll*, the *Public-Pleasing Plump Polish Pumpkin-plumed Bird*, the *Lazy Loose-footed Luxemburgian Luxury Lazuli Bunting*, the *Wonderful Western Austrian Winter Waltzing Bird*, the *Black-beaked Barefooted Baritone Bosnian Bluebird*, the *Cocky Calling Pink-crested Croatian Catbird*, and the *Howling Hungarian Hillbilly Hamster Bird*.

Then there were the *Proud Blue-beret Basque Basketball Bowling Cardinal*, the *Industrious Intelligent Icelandic Arctic Oriole*, the *Fine-feathered Fortunate Faeroese Flaming Flamingo*, the *Bold-and-boisterous Red-headed Irish Potato Bird*, the *Brave Scottish Banner Bagpipe Goldfinch*, the *Wailing White-whiskered Welsh Warbler*, and the *Orange-hooded Olde Queen's Canterbury Talkative English Tea*

Crow. Catchy the Tom-Tom Bird was from the tiny country of Liechtenstein, which is nestled between Switzerland and Austria. His full name was the *Spruce-sitting Purple-crowned Yellow-winged Liechtensteinan Tom-Tom Bird*, because Catchy liked to sit on the branches of the Spruce Tree, an evergreen tree that grows in Liechtenstein and other places in Europe and the world.

Now the competition began. First the *Fancy Golden-throated French Marseille Bird* poured out her glorious song, and all the birds were very impressed by her majestic music. Next the *Double Dirndl-dancing German Green-bellied Bavarian Blackbird* sang a beautiful German folksong that had all the birds clapping their wings and dancing happily. This performance was followed by the enchanting song of the *Lilting Long-tailed Latvian Lavender Lovebird* that all of the birds listened to with fondness and love.

The *Howling Hungarian Hillbilly Hamster Bird* gave an unusual performance of rustic songs from the Hungarian countryside. The gathering was surprisingly refreshed by his contribution. Next were heard the cheerful melodies of the *Yodeling Swiss Eye-ogling Alpine Ostrich.* His birdcall had all the birds laughing with hearty warmth and great merriment.

And so the birds representing the different European countries sang their tunes, one after the other, until everyone was filled with uplifting, sorrowful, joyous, lovely, grand, tender, serene, glad, and touching song. But last of all came Catchy, the *Spruce-sitting Purple-crowned Yellow-winged Liechtensteinan Tom-Tom Bird*, and every*one*—and I mean *every*one, *every single bird*—grew perfectly still. Catchy sat there on the highest branch of an especially tall Spruce Tree, opened his throat, and—full of heart—sang: *Hooeeya hey! Hooeeya hey! Hooeeya volley, hooeeya ney! Fair Liechtenstein, my country mine. Hooeeya hey! Hooeeya ney!*

There wasn't a dry eye in the entire Black Forest. Tears welled up in the eyes of every bird in the crowd, of the *Lean Light-footed Lithuanian Listening Ladybird*, the *Nocturnal Norwegian Northern Nightingale*, the *Multi-colored Czech Castle Courting Chickadee*, the *Elegant Estonian Evergreen Easter Bird*, the *Little Lap Rust-colored*

The Two Tom-Tom Bird Cousins

Reindeer Redpoll, the *Sun-worshipping Serbian Swallow-tailed Sunset Swan*. Even the *Artful Antics Albanian Acting Bird* and the *Slow Slovenly Slovakian Silver-sleeved Stork* wept a few tears, so moving was Catchy's song.

After the judges, a panel of nineteen dignified elderly *Snowy Owls* from a hidden forest in Herzegovina, had met in secret, and the vote was taken, it was unanimously decided that Catchy, the rare *Spruce-sitting Purple-crowned Yellow-winged Liechtensteinan Tom-Tom Bird*, had won the great singing contest. Catchy had won the much-wished-for prize, a trip to far-off China.

Now all of the other European bird representatives wished Catchy well on his adventures, and then each made the journey back to his own country and region. But Catchy caught the next flight to the Orient on *The Asia Wind Express*. Asia, the Orient, is called the Morning Land because the Sun rises each morning in the East, and Asia is the Eastern continent.

Over Austria, Hungary, Romania, Moldova, and Russia he flew. Over the Caspian Sea, Kazakhstan, Uzbekistan, Tajikistan, and Kyrgyzstan he flew until he was over China.

After seven days and seven nights of continuous flight, Catchy finally arrived in the Chinese Province of Szechuan. There he settled down on the highest branch of a Chinese Spruce Tree, whose name is *Veitch's Spruce*, in the middle of the forest near Qingling Mountain for a good day and night's rest after the long journey.

That night Catchy the Tom-Tom Bird dreamed of many things. He dreamed of the great singing contest and the many songs he had heard in the Black Forest. He dreamed of his long flight to China on *The Asia Wind Express* and the breathtaking scenery he had seen from way up high in the sky. But before he awoke on the following morning, Catchy dreamed of his cousin in Asia, who was the only other Tom-Tom Bird in the whole world whom he had never met.

When he awoke, Catchy decided he would try to learn the name of his cousin and of her whereabouts. So he asked all the Chinese birds in the forest around him. None of them knew something. Next he asked the Chinese hares, the forest rabbits, if they had heard anything. But the Chinese hares also knew nothing. So he asked the Chinese squirrels living there, and again with the same result.

Catchy kept on asking and asking. He asked the Chinese forest mice, the Chinese deer, the Chinese ladybugs, the Chinese butterflies, the Chinese beetles, and the Chinese ants. He asked the Chinese white tigers, the Chinese snakes, the Chinese hedgehogs, and the Chinese wild boars. He even asked a *Giant Chinese Panda Bear*. Still, no one had ever heard of an Asian Tom-Tom Bird.

By this time it was nearly sunset, and because he suddenly felt very lonesome in this great Chinese forest, so far away from his beloved home in Liechtenstein, Europe, Catchy began to sing his song, and with more feeling than he ever had before: *Hooeeya hey! Hooeeya hey! Hooeeya volley, hooeeya ney! Fair Liechtenstein, my country mine. Hooeeya hey! Hooeeya ney!*

Then, from the distance, Catchy heard the barely audible song of another bird: *Hooeeya hey! Hooeeya hey! Hooeeya volley, hooeeya ney! Fair China land, my country grand. Hooeeya hey! Hooeeya ney!* When he heard this song, Catchy left his perch atop the Chinese Spruce Tree with great excitement, because he believed the song came from his Asian Tom-Tom Bird cousin.

Catchy flew in the direction of the birdcall about one hundred Spruce Trees to the north, alighted on the top of another *Veitch's Spruce* and sang his song again, and with much enthusiasm: *Hooeeya hey! Hooeeya hey! Hooeeya volley, hooeeya ney! Fair Liechtenstein, my country mine. Hooeeya hey! Hooeeya ney!* Then he became still, eager to hear the song of the other bird. Sure enough it came, and from a distance of only about ten Spruce Trees away: *Hooeeya hey! Hooeeya hey! Hooeeya volley, hooeeya ney! Fair China land, my country grand. Hooeeya hey! Hooeeya ney!*

Catchy was beside himself with joy. He was so overjoyed that he flew the distance of ten Chinese Spruce Trees, landed atop one *Veitch's Spruce* and called out: *Hooeeya hey! Hooeeya hey! Hooeeya volley, hooeeya ney! Catchy's my name, Tom-Tom bird same. Please come to me, to this Spruce Tree. Hooeeya hey! Hooeeya ney!*

The Two Tom-Tom Bird Cousins

Next Catchy heard the sound of a bird flying through the branches. Soon the bird appeared on the Spruce treetop next to his. She was a *Yellow-winged Tom-Tom Bird* like Catchy, but with a blue crown instead of Catchy's purple crown, and at once each recognized his cousin in the other.

They were both so thrilled to see one another that they jumped high up into the air, and flying danced in the sky with glee. Catchy asked his cousin what her name was. She replied, *Matchy's my name, Tom-Tom Bird same*, and the two cousins flew together in the direction of the setting sun, singing in unison, *Hooeeya hey! Hooeeya hey! Hooeeya volley, hooeeya ney! Two Tom-Tom Birds, we sing our words. We cousins are from lands afar. Hooeeya hey! Hooeeya ney!*

Los Angeles
Culver City, California
January 2-4, 2007
Revised Los Angeles
June 30, 2013

The Folk Tale of the
Green Swedish Leprechaun

There once was a green leprechaun named Alex who lived in a forest in Sweden. Alex knew a wise and learned gentleman by the name of Harold who came into his forest to gather berries, nuts, and mushrooms from time to time. This wise man knew many secrets about plants, because he possessed a vast knowledge about herbs, flowers, and all growing things.

One day in the summer, Harold was walking through the forest to find some kantarellar, orange mushrooms that are delicious when sautéed in butter. To assist him, Alex told Harold where a good crop of the kantarellar grew, as they were good friends.

When Harold came to the place Alex had indicated, he saw only holes where the mushrooms had been, because the ugly troll Trapnose had picked and eaten them all up just minutes before the wise man arrived, as the naughty elf Amos had told him of Harold's coming. But Harold was very smart, so he thought of a plan to make Trapnose sick so that the troll would throw up the kantarellar that lay in his big belly.

Soon Harold found Trapnose grinning and picking his nose, and he told him of an intensely wonderful white flower that grew in a clearing on the forest floor that, when eaten, brings much pleasure and intoxication. Trapnose was very powerful, but also stupid, so he walked to the clearing where he found and ate the white flowers, because he loved pleasure above all things.

What Harold did not say was that these intoxicating flowers were mildly poisonous and caused the person who ate them to grow sick to his stomach, and soon Trapnose was heaving until the last of the kantarellar had come up. Then he lay down in the clearing and fell

Reprinted by permission from Alan Lindgren, *Michael and Los Angeles* (Culver City: Sun Sings Publications, 2008), 159–161; and *Kings & Commoners, Mouse, Magic and More* (2011), 121–124.

sound asleep, because the potent white flowers also induced sleepiness.

Next Harold gathered together the kantarellar, now inedible because they had been in Trapnose's stomach. Then the wise man left the forest and spread the spores of the mushrooms over a bed of strawberries in his garden, that lay hundreds of tall tree lengths away, so that new kantarellar would grow there, because he knew that mushrooms are fungi and grow from spores, unlike flowering plants that grow from seeds.

Meanwhile Alex, the spritely Swedish leprechaun, was singing away in a copse of trees in his forest, when naughty Amos appeared and told him of his trickery against Harold. So as to rid himself of Amos's company, Alex said it was none of his business, because he did not like the little elf's ways, but secretly he wished to help Harold. Not knowing that the wise man had already remedied the situation, he devised a plan to do away with Trapnose.

When he found the troll lying asleep snoring loudly in the clearing, Alex took out his small locket that he always wore around his neck, just in case he needed it, and that contained a blinding powder made from the mist of morning fog. He blew the powder onto Trapnose's face, and at once the ugly troll opened his eyes, awakened by the sensation.

"Who disturbs me in my dreams?" Trapnose groaned in a loud voice. "Go back to sleep," said the green leprechaun, now that some of the powder was in the troll's eyes. But when Trapnose closed his eyelids the powder burned his eyes and he could not see.

"Who wishes to fight with me?" bellowed the great troll. "I do," replied Alex, who was now having much fun.

Then the little leprechaun made a spell over Trapnose that sent him reeling out of the clearing and into a large tree trunk, against which the blind troll hit his head, killing him instantly.

When Harold returned to the forest the next day to pick some rare herbs for medicinal teas, he inquired with Alex as to what had become of the troll. When the leprechaun told him everything and as it had happened, the wise gentleman paused for a moment and then said, "Fools mistaken power for strength and wits for wisdom, but they have neither. In four weeks I shall have a good crop of kantarellar from my own garden to enjoy with my wife Frieda.

So, children, be wise like Harold, and do not eat indulgently like the foolish Trapnose, lest you become sick with pleasure. For if you are looking to satisfy your desires, you shall only suffer, but if you are wise you shall enjoy good things in moderation in due course. And that is the tale of Alex, the green Swedish Leprechaun.

Los Angeles
Culver City, California
January 16
February 6, 2008

The Folk Tale of the Little Spanish Cobbler

There once lived a little old Spanish cobbler named Carlos in Barcelona, which is a city in Spain, as you know. He made and repaired shoes, which is what cobblers do, as you know. His clients were mostly the poor and hardworking men and women of Barcelona, and their poor children. One beautiful spring morning a young man entered his shop, which was on a cobblestone street, and asked Carlos how much it would cost to have his shoes repaired.

When he took a close look at the young man's shoes, Carlos replied, "One gold crown, three silver pennies, and a piece of copper." The young man didn't blink an eye and gave the cobbler the money upfront, which means beforehand, as you know.

You see, the old cobbler was actually a wise man, and he could tell that the young man was a very wealthy French prince, because his shoes were so well made, even though he was dressed in ordinary attire, because he didn't want to draw attention to himself, which means he didn't want people to recognize that he was a very wealthy French prince, as you know. The young man asked Carlos when he should return to pick up his shoes, and the little cobbler replied in a fortnight, which is two weeks, as you know. Then the young prince left the shop without saying another word.

Right away Carlos set about repairing the prince's shoes. He used the finest leather and sheepskin in the world, and the most costly gold thread, and he labored and labored nonstop, which means night and day, as you know, for two weeks until the shoes were in perfect condition, even better than when they had been brand new.

When the young prince returned he asked Carlos for his shoes,

Reprinted by permission from Alan Lindgren, *Michael and Los Angeles* (Culver City: Sun Sings Publications, 2008), 161–163; and *Kings & Commoners, Mouse, Magic and More* (2011), 125–127. Also featured in the SPRING 2008 issue (#264) of *Biodynamics*, a publication of the *Bio-Dynamic Farming and Gardening Association, Inc.*

because several important foreign ambassadors were to have an audience with him in the Spanish castle in Barcelona later that same day, which means they were to see him, as you know.

Carlos handed the French prince his shoes and asked him if the shoes were to his liking. After looking them over inside and outside and from all sides, the young man was pleased by the workmanship, so he gave the old cobbler three gold crowns, nine silver pennies, and three pieces of copper more as a tip, much as waitresses receive a handsome tip when they have performed especially good service, as you know. Carlos accepted the money, and the wealthy French prince left the shop wearing the mended shoes, which were in perfect condition, even better than when they had been brand new, as you know.

One week later, when Carlos was hard at work making a set of clogs for a poor client, who walks into his shop but the rich French prince? The little cobbler only looked up from his labors and asked the young man if he could help him.

The prince replied, "I am the Prince of Orleans, soon to inherit the throne of the King of France. When I am crowned King at the palace in Versailles next month, I would like to employ you as my royal cobbler, because you do the finest and best work in your profession. I will pay you a handsome salary."

But Carlos only said, "Good Prince, I am but an old cobbler working in my humble shop here in Barcelona. My clients are all poor like myself, and before you came to me, I had never received more than two pieces of copper to mend a pair of old shoes, and one silver penny to make the finest pair of new shoes. I thank you for your kind offer, but I am content with my life here."

"And if I pay you as much as your heart desires? Then will you join me in Versailles and be my royal cobbler?" the prince persisted.

"Young man, surely you are most generous, but I am quite at home here in my little shop," answered the wise man graciously but unmoved.

"What can I do to make you change your mind?" asked the young prince, who really wanted to employ this skilled old cobbler.

"If you can make it rain five thousand buckets of gold crowns, fifteen thousand buckets of silver pennies, and five thousand buckets of copper pieces on the homes of the poor inhabitants of this town of Barcelona, I will go with you and be your royal cobbler."

The young prince thought for a minute and realized that all of his great riches would be spent on the poor of Barcelona if he did what Carlos asked, so he turned and went away with a sad heart. He could not part with his vast wealth.

Remember children, fine workmanship is like a gift from God, and even the richest prince on earth cannot buy such a gift. And if he could, he would have to give all that he possessed to obtain it, and then he would have given away all his earthly wealth to the poor, which he would never do, because he is too attached to material things.

Los Angeles
Culver City, California
January 16
February 6, 2008

The Folk Tale of Frederick and the Village of Fortune

Many years ago, there lived an old man with his old wife and dog. They lived in an old village, the kind of village where grandmothers used to tell their grandchildren folk fairytales the Brothers Grimm collected and published.

Well, one day, a young nobleman came riding on horseback to this village posthaste. The entire place grew excited as this happened in a small village very rarely. As it turned out, the nobleman was a distant relation to the old woman. When he entered the village, which was called Poverty, the young man asked a small group of villagers who had gathered there where a Mrs. Penniless lived.

Of course, every one in the village of Poverty knew the old woman and where she lived. One man, a good and faithful peasant by the name of Frederick, told the young man he would take him to her dwelling himself. When they arrived, the nobleman dismounted, thanked the peasant with a gold coin, and told him he was free to go. Frederick, wishing it otherwise, petitioned to be present while Mrs. Penniless entertained her rich relative. The young man, who had taken a liking to this honest rustic, consented at once, and soon the two men and the old couple were sitting huddled by the stove in the simple house, while the old dog lay curled up near the stove himself.

Now it should be said that Frederick had gained a certain reputation throughout the region, reaching even the great City, for he had a way with people, and felt equally at ease with the richest men and women as he did with the poorest folk, and he was much beloved by every one. He possessed the virtues had by few, poor or rich, and was

Reprinted with permission from Alan Lindgren, *Kings & Commoners, Mouse, Magic and More* (Culver City: 2011, Sun Sings Publications), 128–142.

known to come from a long line of the wise peasant-folk known in legend as the Marvelous Ones.

They were said to have the gifts of foresight and prophecy, to be Masters of themselves and therewith of all situations, and all those who were born into their ancestral lineage were as respected as they were admired and beloved. But as they were all peasants like Frederick, the Marvelous Ones lived in humble circumstances among the common folk, preferred wholesome company, and cherished simplicity in all things.

Otherwise little was known about them, for want of acquaintance with wisdom, like a veil of secrecy, kept all but shadowed hints and muffled whispers from getting out.

The discussion soon turned to the topic of a large sum of money that the young man explained to the small gathering had been left to the old woman in the will of his wealthy father, who had just died. When he thus informed them of this highly unusual event, even the old dog became interested. Meanwhile, all of the villagers were talking amongst themselves, wondering what the business of the young nobleman with Mrs. Penniless might be.

However, Frederick was entirely unimpressed by this rare piece of news, the likes of which was simply never heard in this village or any other poor village like it. Not only was good Frederick unmoved, he said (and without mincing his words) that this was really unfortunate, and was there any way the money could find another home.

Surprisingly, except for the fact that Frederick was so beloved, and whose opinions were held in such high regard, the old man and his old wife wholeheartedly agreed with the truthful peasant, and they sent the young man away with the money he had brought with him.

The other villagers knew nothing of what had transpired, and as Frederick was renowned to keep a secret, and the old man and woman easily brushed aside all inquiries as to why the rich nobleman had come to see Mrs. Penniless, soon everybody in the village had forgotten about the matter, save an infamous little elf, who lived in a tree hollow in the village square, and who always stuck his nose into every one's business, because he was extremely jealous, and just as greedy. You see the little elf, whose name was Oscar, had secretly followed Frederick and the nobleman when the peasant had taken his new confidante to the humble home of Mrs. Penniless and her husband, and Oscar had seen with his own green eyes the rich young man give Frederick the gold coin and the two of them enter the house.

Try as he would, Oscar was unsuccessful in his attempts at opening the peasant's firmly closed lips, until one fateful unfriendly evening on a cold and windy autumn Sunday, the horrible little elf got Frederick thoroughly drunk, because the wise man had only one weakness, which was a deep and undying love for brew. (After all, he *was* a peasant.)

So, on this particularly cold autumn evening, when Oscar invited Frederick to join him for some of his potent urchin ale in the hollow of the notorious tree where he lived, it didn't take any coaxing for the greedy little elf to accomplish what he had set out to do.

Soon the two unlikely companions were having a rousing good time (at least Frederick was), and devious Oscar made sure his guest had had as much of the strong brew as his lusty peasant heart desired, which was so much that Frederick was bowled over with laughter at any and every thing his mean host said.

Then Oscar knew to put the essential question, and he smiled a repugnant but ingratiating smile at Frederick, and asked in a speciously saccharine tone of voice, just what was the business of the young nobleman who had ridden on horseback into the village of Poverty to the Pennilesses.

By this time Frederick felt really chummy with this utterly unlikable elf, and he replied with much enthusiasm that the rich young man had brought a huge amount of money to Mrs. Penniless that his dead father had bequeathed to her in his will, as you well know.

When, on further questioning, the scrounging elf learned that Frederick had convinced the old couple to turn the fortune down, sending it back with the young nobleman (as you well know), Oscar grew furious, and ordered good but totally inebriated Frederick out of his tree house.

Frederick and the Village of Fortune

Frederick, now in jovial spirits, merely slapped the spiteful elf on his small back and genially asked for another large mug of the brew, but this only infuriated his host the more. Frederick, feeling himself in most pleasant company, could not be deterred, and the by-now enraged Oscar turned from his usual invidious green a bright red, and he stormed out of his tree into the cold night, for it had by this time grown very late.

Good Frederick, seeing that his little false friend had deserted him, helped himself to a few more filled-to-the-brim mugs of the ale, and then he left the tree himself, staggering out into the nippy night air. The chill had an awakening effect, but only enough to get him home, and he made his way to his own quarters, passing out on his straw bed where he lay sound asleep snoring loudly until he woke up at noon two days later.

When he stood up, Frederick went over to his washbasin and doused his grubby face with cold water. Try as he would, he could not remember what had taken place in the tree, only that Oscar had gotten him completely drunk. Meanwhile, the up-to-no-good elf had calmed down enough to devise a plan, his pallor had returned to its usual disgusting green, and he was on his way to the great City.

You see, Oscar had learned from his unwary guest that the nobleman lived in the glittering Metropolis, so he set out at once to find him to connive his way into an unethical agreement or partnership that would transfer the will into *his* name whereby *he* would inherit the fortune and the money would land into *his* hands.

When he arrived in the proud and beautiful City, the clever elf soon learned the whereabouts of the young man's mansion, for he had a way of finding out most anything he wished to know, so accomplished and refined his nosiness had become through many years foul practice.

When he came to the great doors of the mansion, and the old butler had answered the bell, diminutive Oscar had to verily shout to be heard. But when his repulsive voice echoed throughout the huge house, the young nobleman himself came downstairs to see who it was who had disturbed the peace that always reigned there.

When he only saw a little green elf, the rich young man smiled, and politely inquired with this small person what it was that he wished with him. Oscar motioned to the wealthy nobleman to listen to his ulterior tidings privately, and thinking nothing was amiss, the young man offered him a seat in the anteroom where visitors were invited to wait. Then the rich lord leaned over from his chair and lent the cunning elf his ear.

Now Oscar took advantage of his opportunity, and he whispered that he was a close relation to Mrs. Penniless, that the old woman had given him full rights to her inheritance, that she had just died and, for the grand *finale*, the smart elf produced two parchments he begged the nobleman to unseal and read.

The gracious host acquiesced and did as Oscar had asked, but after he patiently read the convincing official-looking death certificate and deed that supposedly transferred the entire bequest into the elf's covetous little hands, he only explained that the money had already been given to another poor relation who was also named in the will, and whose inheritance had thereby quadrupled. There was nothing he or any one could do for the elf.

"But this is an outrage!" cried Oscar. "The money belongs to *me*. My auntie Mrs. Penniless inherited it, and she signed the whole sum over to yours truly. These are her words and her signature!" The nobleman, understanding the elf's intentions, quietly repeated the conversation he had had with the Pennilesses and Frederick. He had nothing to hide and said the matter was already settled.

Well, it was clear to the impudent elf there wasn't a thing he could do to change the situation to his favor, so he took back the two false parchments and bade the rich young man farewell.

But just as he was about leave, Oscar said (as in passing) that he had business to do with the very relation who had been given Mrs. Penniless's fortune, and would his noble host be so kind as to direct him to their residence.

The young man was very friendly and told the tricky elf of a very small village by the name of Fortune that lies far away on the other side of the City, and where a certain Mrs. Providence lived. Then Oscar bowed and thanked the good lord and took his leave.

At once he took off in search of the village, whose name and general whereabouts he had just learned, and he thought he was well on his way there. As it was late and nightfall, Oscar decided he would find an inn where he could sleep and resume his journey to riches in the morning. When he came on just such a place, the deceitful elf rang the bell, and an old innkeeper answered. Oscar asked the man how much he charged for a single room for one night, and he paid the full amount upfront in *fool's gold* and retired to bed, where he soon lay in a deep sleep.

Oscar dreamed of many things that night. Some of his dreams were muddled and indecipherable, and some were weird and strange, some were ugly and nightmarish, but those he awoke with were very pleasant, for they showed him a lavish palace with stockpiles of gold, silver, and diamonds; and costly silk, lace, jewelry, and dining ware; and other precious items.

At sunrise he was up and refreshed. Eager to get to his destination, the crafty elf asked the old innkeeper the direction of the village of Fortune. Then he trudged off, his mind set on meeting this Mrs. Providence, his greedy little hands already fidgeting with selfish elfish delight for what he believed they would be in possession of before sundown.

Now it so happened that the countryside on this side of the great City was quite different from that where he came from, and where the poor village of Poverty in whose dirty square his tree home grew was situated. You see, this other countryside was magical because its fields were filled with riddles, where men's fortunes were made and broken, its farmers sowed questions and harvested answers in three minutes, its wonderful villages housed miracles, and its villagers knew all things.

Even the innkeeper knew much, for example that Oscar had paid him in *fool's gold*, because his inn was between the ostentatious Metropolis and this countryside, so he had already discovered who Oscar really was, and what Oscar really wanted.

Because it was so beautiful here, Oscar found himself extremely happy, and he decided to prolong his journey by a few days just to enjoy the lovely scenery, riding on an oxcart instead of by horse-and-buggy.

But as he did not know the fields were full of riddles, and the farmers sowed questions and harvested answers (in three minutes), Oscar did not have a clue as to why the countryside was so stunning, which it was because it was magical. Nor did the elf know that the Marvelous One Frederick, whom he thought was native to his own region, actually came from a miraculous village in this countryside, and that he therefore knew all things.

So when, on the third day of his trip on the oxcart, Oscar saw a quaint village by the name of Marvelous that was on a stream, he hadn't a clue that this was where Frederick was from, or that the wise peasant was there at this very moment, because he could travel from the village of Poverty on the other side of the dazzling City to his home village of Marvelous in this countryside is exactly three days, or that he had done so because he knew of Oscar's coming, because he knew all things.

When Oscar jumped off the oxcart to have a drink of water from the stream, the intent little elf decided he would find out how close he was to the tiny village of Fortune where Mrs. Providence lived. After he had thoroughly quenched his thirst, he entered the village of Marvelous and asked the first person he saw his question.

This was an experienced farmer by the name of Browning, who replied he would go at once and find out, and that he would return in five minutes. Then Oscar sat down on a bumpy rock in the village of Marvelous, and waited.

Meanwhile Browning, the old farmer, who like all of the villagers in Marvelous was a Marvelous One, walked out into his field and sowed Oscar's question. In exactly three minutes Browning harvested the answer, and he returned to the village after a total of exactly five minutes and told the green elf the answer to his question, just as he had said he would.

Frederick and the Village of Fortune

But Oscar was so delighted by this enchanting village of Marvelous that he could not bring himself to depart at once, rather he decided to stay and spend the night there, and resolved to resume his journey to teeny Fortune in the morning, that he believed he would reach by nightfall that day.

So the gritty little elf asked Browning where he might be put up for the night, saying he was glad to pay for a small supper, the use of a warm bed, and a hearty breakfast in the morning, to prepare himself for his continued journey. Browning said he knew of just such a villager who would be amenable to this, and that he would accompany him to the peasant's house himself to make sure he was at home. This was none other than Frederick's place.

When they arrived at the trusty peasant's home, Frederick was not at home, because he was out in the fields plowing riddles, and making and breaking men's fortunes. But Browning said, and to Oscar's relief, he was sure the peasant wouldn't mind if the elf went inside to wait for his return, and that he himself would join him.

Soon the old farmer and the envious elf had made themselves quite cozy in Frederick's house, which wasn't as small as one might have thought (for only one man). There were two wooden chairs, a handsome wood table, a hand-carved wooden bench, two rustic beds, a wash basin, and a cord of wood by a stone hearth, where Browning and Oscar made a small fire and warmed themselves while they waited for Frederick.

They spoke of the weather, and how pleasant it was (even in the evening after it had cooled off), how picturesque the countryside was, and just how nice it was to be here.

Just before sunset, in walks Frederick carrying a bundle of answers to questions he had sown that morning, that he hadn't had time to harvest earlier, because he had been occupied plowing the fields full of riddles, and making and breaking men's fortunes. Goodly Frederick set down the large bundle of answers in the corner of the room next to a broom, and then seated himself on the beautifully carved wooden bench.

Now you would have thought that Oscar, with his sharp green eyes, would have recognized the kindly peasant, because he was so used to seeing him around the village square in Poverty where he lived in his tree.

But Frederick looked different in Marvelous on this side of the big City than he did where Oscar had always seen him, because here the people all looked very handsome and beautiful, and if they did on the other side of the City, then they looked only more so here. In addition, Frederick was wearing different clothes here, and his coat and boots were as golden as the marvelous fields, his hat and gloves as charming as the roads and oxcarts here.

Also, this village Marvelous housed miracles, so everything was placed in a different light here, just as was the case in all the villages of this magical countryside. What's more Marvelous was a very old village where it was said the Marvelous Ones had lived for many centuries, and where wonders never ceased, so the reliable peasant was among his own kith and ken, and thus felt truly at home here, where he was born and raised, and where he had received his schooling into the secrets of the Marvels.

In short, Frederick was on his home terrain, and he simply did not look the same in magical wonderful Marvelous as he did in poor pitiable Poverty.

At any rate, Oscar did not recognize Frederick, but Frederick did recognize the mischievous elf, and, after introductions, Browning bade the host and his little guest a good evening and departed to his own house where his patient wife awaited him.

Oscar gave Frederick a *fool's gold* coin for food and lodgings, which the peasant full-knowing accepted, simply because he was so kind and good-willed, and Frederick prepared a warm supper of goose stew that he served with hot buttered whole-riddled rolls and nice hot minty tea, and before too long the two fellows had eaten their fill and gone to bed.

By ten o'clock the next morning, when Oscar awakened, dependable Frederick had already left as he had business to attend to in the countryside on the other side of the City, but the trusty peasant had left his disagreeable little guest a generous breakfast of wild boar bacon and fried quail eggs (sunny-side up, just the way Oscar liked them), with magic corn toast smeared with freshly-churned golden butter and wondrous red currant jam, and to drink a large mug of rich hot coffee with whipped goat cream and creamy crystallized honey (Oscar's favorite), and by twelve noon the elf had eaten his full and climbed onto the back of an oxcart headed straight for the tiny hamlet of Fortune.

Because of a sudden flash flood, which was followed by three hours of very light drizzling rain, and dozens of wonderful double rainbows, Oscar's entry into Fortune was delayed by one more day, and just before the oxcart he boarded on the next morning entered the village outskirts at sunset, Frederick had arrived first and was visiting with old Mrs. Providence, who had just inherited the huge sum of money (quadrupling her original inheritance), who, however, remained with her old husband in this unheard of and insignificant village of Fortune as before their good fortune befell them.

When Oscar found a farmer mending his plow in the miniature village square, he inquired with the man where a Mrs. Providence lived. Expecting to find a luxurious villa, Oscar was surprised when he was brought to the humble cottage where the old woman lived with Mr. Providence.

Eager to speak with her, the ever-nosy elf forgot to thank the farmer who had shown him to the house, and instead stuck his nose into a crack in the weathered wall to see if he could learn something and anything about the woman that he could use to gain access to her money.

He did not find what he was looking for, but what Oscar *did* see was even better, for there sat Mr. and Mrs. Providence with the young nobleman and Frederick by the stove warming their hands, deep in conversation. Knowing he *had* to hear what they were discussing, Oscar quietly walked around to the back of the cottage where he had noticed a window, and he managed to open it just enough to slip into the house unheard. Before you can say "Inheritance", Oscar had tip-toed behind their backs and, filled with expectation, he clearly heard the young nobleman say the following:

"A small green elf showed up at my mansion in the City one week ago demanding Mrs. Penniless's inheritance. I explained the money had already been transferred into your hands. When he asked me where he could find the party, I directed him here."

By now Oscar was so excited it was very difficult for him to contain himself. He looked all about him to see whether he could figure out where the money might be kept.

"But did you tell him my advice to Mrs. Providence?" Frederick went on.

It was then that Oscar realized that this was none other than Frederick the peasant, whom he had gotten drunk to learn of Mrs. Penniless's inheritance, and who was the selfsame peasant whom he had stayed with and been so well fed by in Marvelous two days before.

Now he was very nearly bursting with anticipation to learn what would be said next. So it was with bated breath that he listened to the following:

"Do you mean," the old woman asked, "do you mean that inheriting such a sum of money is a most unlucky thing?"

"That is what I said," Frederick continued.

"No," the young man replied. "The elf was so eager to find you (and here he indicated the old couple) that he departed before I could mention it."

Frederick and the Village of Fortune

Oscar became very agitated at this point, but, unable to pull himself away from the urgent conversation, he kept eavesdropping, transfixed.

"Well," Mr. Providence went on, completing the thought. "When the elf gets here, he will soon learn that we turned down the unpromising inheritance, although no one in the entire village of Fortune—or in the entire countryside, for that matter—knows, except for the five of us."

You see, the villagers on this side of the City *did* know everything.

"Darn, darn, darn, darn, darn, darn, darn, darn," muttered Oscar to himself as he walked in little circles, going quite mad. Then, more loudly,

"Darn! Darn! Darn! Darn! Darn! Darn! Darn! Darn!"

"Is that you, Oscar?"

Frederick asked, knowing but concerned, turning around to see the crazed elf marching around in ever-smaller circles as he quickly lost his sanity.

"Frederick broke my fortune, Frederick broke my fortune," was all the frenzied elf could say.

Oscar tied himself into such a knot that neither he, nor any one else could untwist. And so he remains to this day. And that is the tale of Frederick and the Village of Fortune.

Los Angeles
September 7-12, 2009

A Story for Ages 3–6 Years

The Three Brothers

The Three Brothers

There once lived three boys in a house. The oldest one was named Peter. Peter was nine years old. The middle one was called James, and James was six years old. The little one was named Stevie, and he was only three years old. Peter, James, and Stevie were brothers. They lived in the house by themselves because their parents, John and Cynthia Thompson, had gone away to the country one day and had never returned. So Peter, being the eldest, took care of his younger brothers. He made sure they were well fed and kept warm in the cold weather with blankets, sweaters, scarves, hats, and mittens.

One day, when the three brothers were all seated at the dinner table eating their supper, which was meatloaf, potatoes, peas, and carrot cake, little Stevie began to cry. He cried and cried and cried, and the tears kept flowing from his blue eyes and would not stop. Peter asked his younger brother what was the matter.

"Stevie," he said. "Why are you crying?"

"Mommy and Daddy have left us here in the big house and are never coming home," Stevie answered.

And then the little boy continued crying, and even more than before.

Next James, the middle brother, said to little Stevie,

"Stevie. We are all right here. Peter takes good care of us. He makes sure we stay warm when it's cold and that we have enough

Reprinted with permission from Alan Lindgren, *Kings & Commoners, Mouse, Magic and More* (Culver City: Sun Sings Publications, 2011), 177–183.

food to eat."

Here James pointed to the meatloaf, the potatoes, the peas, and the carrot cake.

"See, Stevie," James said. "What a good meal we have!"

But little Stevie only kept on crying, and even more than before.

Soon the dinner table was covered in tears, and the tears formed a brook, and the brook became a stream, and the stream became a river that flowed right through the house. Before you could blink an eye, Peter, James, and Stevie were taken up by the river of tears and began floating along the flowing water on top of the dining room table and out of the house.

Peter made sure his two younger brothers were safe. He stood up on the table and held one of James's hands and one of Stevie's hands. Then he had James and Stevie hold one another's hand. Sometimes the dinner table almost tipped over, but then it straightened itself and became sure and stable again.

The boys passed by many houses as they floated through the town carried along by the flowing river of tears. Then they floated right out of the town and into a dark forest. In the forest they could not see because it was too dark. Peter took out a large candle from his coat pocket that he always carried for emergencies. He lit the candle and now the three brothers could see.

They saw forest rabbits, forest mice, forest toads, forest bears, and even forest faeries. The forest faeries that they saw were dancing on their faerie mound. On the faerie mound forest toadstools and forest mushrooms grew.

"Help us!"

Peter called out to the dancing faeries as the table the boys were standing on floated by the faerie mound. One of the faeries, Andrew by name, jumped up onto the dinner table and cast a little spell that stopped the river from flowing. Little Stevie was so surprised that he stopped crying, and soon all of his tears had dried up and the river was no more.

Now Peter, James, and Stevie were standing on top of the dining room table holding hands next to a forest faerie named Andrew on a faerie mound in the middle of a dark forest. Andrew waved his left hand. Now they could see in the forest. Stevie asked Andrew where his parents were because he missed them so.

"Where are my parents?" the little boy cried out.

But before he could begin crying tears again, Andrew told the three brothers to follow him. So the four of them jumped off the dinner table and onto the faerie mound and began walking through the forest. Now they saw fun squirrels and merry birds, friendly dwarves and tiny ants, magic deer and golden hives with honeybees, great rocks to climb on and many beautiful trees.

Soon they came to a great palace made of pearls.

"How beautiful!" James said when they saw the shining palace.

"Who lives there?" asked Peter.

"The Queen of the faeries lives there," replied Andrew.

And the four of them walked right up to the front gates of the palace that were made of pure gold.

Andrew knocked on the golden gates three times and the gates opened. In the little group strode until they came to the front door of the palace, which was made of rose bark and rosewood.

Andrew knocked on the door three times and the door opened. Then the little group entered the palace into a great hall where dozens of faeries were walking busily about, taking notes in notebooks.

"What are the palace faeries taking notes about?" asked James.

"O, they're taking notes for the Queen," Andrew replied.

Little Stevie bumped into one of the faeries who was taking notes. The little boy asked the palace faerie where his parents were.

"Where are my Mommy and Daddy? They left the house one day, and now we don't know where to find them," he said.

The palace faerie absentmindedly pointed to a small wooden door in the corner of the great hall and walked on, busily taking notes for the Queen. Here Andrew, the forest faerie, left the three brothers, saying he had business to take care of in the forest.

Before Peter could ask him what they should do next, a big fat faerie opened the small wooden door in the corner of the great hall and, barely squeezing through, disappeared into the other side. Next Peter told his two younger brothers to follow him. He took James and Stevie's hands, and together they went through the open wooden door to the other side.

Dozens of fat faeries were seated on benches around a long table quickly eating turkey with mashed potatoes and gravy, stuffing, cranberry sauce, and pumpkin pie. As their plates emptied, fresh food appeared, so the fat faeries kept eating without a break.

James was hungry from their long journey, so he asked one particularly plump faerie if he and his two brothers could join them at the table. All of the fat faeries on one side of the long table moved down the bench to make room for them, and soon the three brothers were eating beside them.

After they had stuffed themselves on turkey, mashed potatoes, gravy, stuffing, cranberry sauce, and pumpkin pie, little Stevie remembered that he hadn't found his parents, and he was just about to cry. Who entered the dining room from a small chamber but the Queen of the faeries herself! Little Stevie was so surprised that he forgot all about crying.

Now Peter went bravely up to the Queen and said:

"O, Queen. My two brothers and I have been on a long journey looking for our parents, who left home one morning and never returned. Can you help us find them?"

Here the Queen sat down on her royal purple velvet seat, took little Stevie onto her lap, and began to sing:

> "Brothers three and brothers boys
> Where, o where your children's joys?
> You are come without your toys
> Where your parents life enjoys."

Next the Queen put little Stevie back down next to her royal seat and snapped her fingers three times. Who entered the dining room from the small chamber but John and Cynthia Thompson, Peter, James, and Stevie's parents? Little Stevie was so happy that he laughed out loud, ran up to them and said,

"Mommy and Daddy! You're safe! We will never let you go away again!"

The father and mother hugged their three sons, and the family remained in the Queen's palace where they all lived happily ever after.

Los Angeles
July 10, 2008
Revised December 2, 2010
Further revised July 1, 2013

Seven Stories for Youth and Adults

The Sailor and the Bum—A Short Story

The Bonfire—A Story Within and Story

Jonathan and Anastasia—An Anthropomorphist Story

Johnson's New Friend—A Short Story for Ages 9 and up

Stevenson and the Books—A Short Story

Man and Baby—A Short Story

Martha—A Story

The Sailor and the Bum

There was a sailor, young, robust, and bold. He led a life filled with gusto, such a one that others could only gape in awe at his style. Now nearby the homeport of this sailor, there lived a bum. This bum had roughly the same build as the sailor, and was identical in height and weight, even in hair and eye color. But the bum had little gusto for life; he just made it from one day to the next.

Now there was a rumor among the fisher-folk of the community that this sailor famous for his gusto and this well-known local bum were actually twin brothers, separated at infancy by unusual destiny. The child who became the bum was left one day sunning on the porch in a pretty basket when someone snatched him away and left him in the poor district, far away. The child who became the robust sailor was then spoiled, for his mother lavished all the things on him she wanted to shower upon her other, lost son.

The stolen child was soon adopted by a poor family with only the pretty basket for identification, well cared for, but under meager circumstances, and thus was not encouraged to grow in the beneficial atmosphere of education and culture. He developed no interest in the pursuit of goals as a child and followed himself in this way into adulthood, when he took up his abode as a bum in the poor district of town, while spending his free time by the sea.

The well-raised child blossomed under the wholesome care of family and society. It was an educated people, and schooling was fundamental, with cultural events holding a central place in the weekly gatherings of the community. He became a famous and much-

Reprinted with permission from Alan Lindgren, *The Magic of the Stars* (Culver City: 2004 and 2005, Sun Sings Publications), 190–191; and *Kings & Commoners, Mouse, Magic and More* (2011), 187–189.

much-beloved sailor, favored by man, woman, and child alike.

On the outskirts there lived the fisher-folk who believed many things considered peculiar by the wealthy folk and odd by those in the poor district. They believed, among other things, that persons with a deeper tie to one another find themselves united by life's unusual circumstances, and they believed that these two young men were true brothers whose reuniting would someday come about.

The bum wandered frequently through the port area, for he enjoyed the liveliness there with all of the boats docking and sailing away, the many people, the birds in great abundance, and especially the sea. Indeed, he frequently saw his unknown-to-him brother, though with no especial interest.

The sailor lived a grand and adventurous life, with many long trips by ship to distant and foreign lands. Each time he returned, he brought with him tales of his journeys for his family and friends in the town. He was a tall and handsome man, strong and well tanned from his work aboard ship.

As the rumor spread that these two young men, worlds apart, were really twin brothers, their mother tried desperately to find some sign, something which would, bearing witness, confirm what the fisher-folk had long known.

The bum had nothing helpful to say; he could not remember back to the time he had been left sunning out on the porch. The sailor was doubtful, to say the least, for their physical resemblance was well covered over by their habit, so now the ageing mother went in search of the home of the unfortunate brother. Into the poor district, door-to-door, she asked whether a son had been adopted at such and such a time years before.

One day she came upon a door ajar. As she went up the broken steps to inquire within, she saw a worn old basket lying on the porch, and she paused. This basket, despite its condition, resembled precisely the two she had purchased for her twins over twenty years before.

Just then an old woman stepped out from the little house, inviting her into conversation. Word by word, the two women uncovered the binding significance of the basket, even to the point of establishing the common date when the basket with its contents was taken and deposited in the street by this house. Joyful, the two women went out, each to find the child she had so lovingly raised to bring him the good news.

At the port a sailing ship had just docked. Easy to spot was the robust son as he boldly ambled down the planks. There came the bum, now beaming with fresh news of his brotherhood. The two brothers shared each other, one to the other, united together for the rest of their lives.

Culver City, California
May 1987
Inglewood, California
August 2004
Los Angeles
July 2013

The Bonfire

Directly after the party, the guests decided they would walk to the beach to celebrate the first night of summer with a great bonfire. So they turned to the left and took a side street where hardly a soul was to be found, so that they could enjoy the quiet and the fresh night air. When they arrived at the beach, one older couple left because they wanted to spend the night alone together, but the others, three young couples, a tall bachelor, two bachelorettes, a young widow in her mid thirties, and a learned gentleman (age about fifty), proceeded to gather kindling and firewood, which is to say driftwood, from the surrounding area near the neighboring pier, which was deserted as it had grown cool, roughly 40° Fahrenheit.

The time was 10:30pm, and soon the company had amassed enough driftwood for a good-sized bonfire. The bachelor had brought a satchel filled with deli sandwiches made with various meats and cheeses, and the widow carried a large picnic basket laden with pastries of all sorts, and bottles of juice and wine, and with mugs as well. Fortunately the older gentleman, a dignified professor, smoked a pipe, and thus carried matches with his pipe tobacco. After they had piled the wood high, he lit the kindling, and soon the fire was burning brightly in the surrounding darkness, the colorful flames dancing and leaping in the breezy air.

Everyone was warming his hands and standing near the bonfire. The couples held each other, and the bachelorette girls snuggled up to the tall bachelor like two turtledoves. By this time the widow had her arm around the professor, so that each helped to keep the other warm. The sandwiches and pastries were quietly passed around, the wine or

Reprinted with permission from Alan Lindgren, *Kings & Commoners, Mouse, Magic and More* (Culver City: Sun Sings Publications, 2011), 191–199.

juice poured to the liking of each one, and as everyone cuddled up to one another eating and sipping their food and drinks, the professor took out his pipe and introduced himself in a warm rich baritone, saying he was going to tell them a strange tale.

"There once lived three sisters in a small apartment," he began. "The eldest was a thirty-six year-old spinster and a compulsive seamstress, ever sewing curtains and dresses for clients, and mending old clothes. She disliked the world, which is to say the company of society, and so depended on her two younger sisters for companionship. Although she was not easy to get along with, the three sisters were all very close."

Here the professor paused and lit his pipe, inhaling deeply, then blowing out puffs of the sweetly smelling smoke in concentric rings.

"The middle sister," he went on, "was the dependable one. She was at age thirty employed as a secretary in a large law firm in the city and earned a tidy sum. She had been seeing the same man for the past nine years, and they were engaged for the last three of them, but neither was ever quite ready to marry, so they agreed to wait for the right time, which lay somewhere in the indefinite future.

"The youngest sister, at twenty-two, was very beautiful and sensitive, and had a lovely soprano voice. She sang in several church choirs for pay, and was often heard giving a solo. Indeed, those who frequented concerts in the area were well-acquainted with her true sweet voice, which poured forth exquisite song through two pretty lips, and which gave expression to her beautiful soul that was housed in an equally attractive figure.

"She often went out on dates with handsome and talented young men who aspired to be famous artists, architects, poets, and composers, just as she hoped one day to sing on the renowned stages of the great venues in the big cities across the country. Unlike these young men, however, she was not merely a talent, rather possessed a true gift in her voice, and was destined to be discovered and earn a place in the hearts of many thousands worldwide.

"Now one gloomy evening in November, after a particularly boring day at the office, the middle sister, whose name was Doris, decided to stop by the grocery store to pick up a dozen carnations to brighten up their flat. But after she had selected and purchased the flowers, and was leaving the market to go to her car, an older gentleman of about sixty-five years with thick glasses bumped into her as he was looking down.

He had lost his wallet on a nearby street over half an hour earlier and was trying to find it. At once Doris dropped the bouquet, falling down onto the sidewalk breaking her right arm.

"Soon the paramedics were there to take her to the emergency room. Addresses were exchanged, the old gentleman forgot what he was doing and where he was going, and Doris, badly shaken, was taken to the local hospital, which was nearby.

"Meanwhile Marie, the youngest sister, was walking quickly down the next street over. She saw her former boyfriend, a handsome twenty-five year-old artist named Peter, walking in the opposite direction on the other side of the street, and she waved to him.

"Marie was just about to call out his name, when he stepped down from the sidewalk into the street to recover a wallet someone had dropped, thinking to locate the man to return it to him. But Peter never saw Marie, for a taxicab driver hit him head-on, and he was killed instantly.

"Now Frieda, who was the eldest of the three, and the spinster seamstress, was sitting upstairs in their apartment at her sewing machine, finishing up some expensive curtains for a well-to-do client, when the telephone rang. 'Well,' she exclaimed to herself, set aside her work, and picked up the receiver. The person on the other end of the line asked in a familiar voice, 'Frieda, is that you?'

Frieda paused, because she almost recognized the voice, though she couldn't quite place it.

"Slowly, as though in a trance, she replied, 'Yes, this is Frieda,' and she dropped the receiver, collapsing on the floor from a heart attack. 'Frieda,' the voice kept on. 'Frieda, this is your cousin Fionn. Frieda, are you there?'

"At this very moment, Doris was being examined by a doctor, who was both efficient and excellent. He told her that her right ulna—a bone in the forearm—had sustained a slight fracture. He went on to explain that her entire right arm would have to be put in a cast after minor surgery to align the bone properly, and that the skin would not have to be broken as this would be an external manipulation only. The fracture would completely heal in six weeks, and there would be no permanent damage.

"At this same time Marie, still standing where she had been when she saw the accident, was crying uncontrollably, while Peter's body was wrapped in a sheet and taken away in an ambulance to the morgue. She was one of three people who had witnessed the accident, but was the only one who knew Peter personally.

"The taxicab driver stood outside of his cab in shock, unable to speak when the police questioned him as to what had happened. It was later revealed the accident was not his fault, but only a tragedy with no one to blame.

"The wallet was identified as belonging to a Malcolm Charles Alberts, who happened to be the gentleman with the thick glasses who had accidentally caused Doris's right arm to be broken the next block over. Marie was asked where she lived so that she could be accompanied by a police officer safely home."

At this point the professor slightly shifted his weight, while thoughtfully dusting off some sand that had blown onto the widow's dress, who was by this time entranced like the others by the tale, while comfortably hugging the strong storyteller's chest which vibrated warmly as he spoke.

"Meanwhile," the professor continued, "Frieda had identified the voice as belonging to her cousin Fionn, and she somehow managed to find and pick up the receiver, which was hanging dangling by the cord. She held it to her mouth and said in a weak voice, 'Fionn. I've just had a heart attack. It's a mild one I think. But I'm all alone in the apartment now, and I need to see a doctor.'

"Now Fionn, who lived over a thousand miles away in Boston, happened to be in town on a business trip, and this was the reason she'd phoned, thinking she would stop by to see her three cousins. She was very good at handling emergencies, because she'd worked in a hospital for a decade years earlier. So she said, 'Frieda. Don't move. I'm nearby. I'll call an ambulance and be by your side in minutes.'

"Doris had by this time been wheeled into the operating room. She was still upset by the whole ordeal, but had already calmed down considerably, because she had adjusted to the reality of her situation, and had resolved to make the best of things.

"She already had plans how she would spend her recuperation, teaching herself to write using her left hand, as she was right-handed. She would then be able to write relatives more frequently, something she had wanted to do, but hadn't had the time to. With these thoughts in her mind, she was put under general anesthetic for the surgery.

"Marie arrived at the flat just minutes after the paramedics and Fionn, which was a good thing, because seeing her sister lying on the floor would have been too much for her to handle. Fionn assured Marie Frieda would be okay, although she didn't know this herself, but to calm and comfort her.

"After they saw Frieda taken safely to the hospital, which was the very same institution where Doris was in surgery at that very moment, Marie again remembered the sudden death of Peter, and she wept uncontrollably in fits, her whole body shuddering as she relived the scene in her mind, unable to turn her attention to the present moment. This except when Fionn interrupted her vivid nightmare with news about the family back home in Massachusetts.

"Shortly thereafter, Marie agreed to go with Fionn to the hospital to be by Frieda's bedside in order to comfort her, and already this thought helped Marie regain some composure and grounding in the moment.

"Fionn thought to leave a note for Doris, and neither suspected they would find her in the same hospital, because Marie had lost track of the time and the regular schedule that Doris always abided by, by which she should have been home forty-five minutes earlier.

"As Marie was fidgeting nervously in the passenger seat of her cousin's rental car, Fionn tried to distract her and lighten the situation by relating recent events of the family back in Boston, where they had all grown up together, and where Fionn still spent her time when she wasn't away on business, which was all-too-often those days.

"Although Marie wasn't paying any attention to Fionn's chatter, because she was toying with her bracelet, similar to a small child who is oblivious to its environment in its own fantasy world, her cousin's voice was pleasant and had a calming effect, making her feel safe and protected.

"Meanwhile at the hospital, Doris was already out of surgery wearing a well-made but heavy cast on her right arm, and she woke up from her anesthetized state somewhat dazed. At first she was confused and, although she never would have admitted it, frightened, but then she remembered her fall, the doctor's examination and explanation, and her plans to pass the time during recuperation, and once again she was back to her old, matter-of-fact self.

"Frieda, on the other hand, was still quite weak, and although the doctors believed she would recover from the heart attack, she would have to be watched and cared for the rest of her life, and never left alone in case another cardiac arrest should occur, as her heart was in poor condition.

"Now Fionn and Marie had just arrived at the hospital, and Fionn inquired at the reception as to the whereabouts of the emergency room. On their way walking through the corridors of the hospital to visit Frieda they came upon Doris, cast and all, who was being transported to the main floor to rest for a few days and receive physical therapy before discharge.

It was Doris who saw Fionn and Marie first with her sharp eyes. When Doris called out: 'Well, I just had a little accident. Was knocked down by an old man, half-blind. It's nothing, really. Don't mind the cast. I'll teach myself to use my left hand to catch up on my correspondence, read, and such,' Marie completely returned to herself. It was the sound of her sister's voice that made her feel right and good and 'normal' as she quickly walked up to the gurney and gave Doris a kiss on the cheek.

"'And look who's here,' Doris said pointedly. 'Fionn Alberts. What brings you here?' So Fionn had to talk about Frieda and the heart attack, and that Frieda was in emergency right at this moment, and that she and Marie were on their way to be with her.

"'Is Frieda going to be alright?' Doris was concerned, and this showed in her voice. 'She's so young to have a heart attack. Do give her my love, and tell her I'll be over to visit her as soon as the doctors will allow me.'

"While Doris and Fionn were exchanging these words, Marie grew distraught once again. First she remembered seeing her eldest sister Frieda being taken away by the paramedics to the hospital, and then the terrible accident and death of her young boyfriend Peter came before her eyes, and she began to cry, shaking all over, unable to control herself.

"On seeing this Doris asked Marie, "What is it darling? Baby,' for this was how she often addressed her baby sister of whom she was so fond, 'Are you okay?' Marie shook her head. Her sister coaxed her into talking with the words, 'Sweetheart, trust your sister. It will do your heart good.'

"Marie looked up and confessed, 'Peter—you remember my boyfriend, the artist I dated—he was hit and killed by a taxicab right before my eyes!' And she began to weep again. But somehow sharing this with Doris comforted her, and she took a few deep breaths and slowly began to relax. Doris sensed right away that her younger sister still needed her to be close, so she said, 'Marie. Why don't you go with me to my new room and keep me company for a while? I don't know anyone in this big hospital, and it would cheer me up.' When Fionn agreed with Doris, encouraging her to spend some time with her middle sister, Marie quietly consented, and she walked alongside the gurney as the orderly wheeled Doris to her hospital room. Then Fionn asked further directions to Frieda's room in emergency, and went on ahead alone.

"All this was long ago," said the kind professor, putting his pipe away.

"But what happened to the sisters?" one of the bachelorettes, still clinging to the tall bachelor, asked intently.

"Yes," they all chimed in, "what happened to Frieda—and Doris—and Marie?"

"Frieda?" said the professor. "She was nursed by another of their cousins, Fionn's older sister Monica, until her death at age sixty from a heart attack. And Doris? She finally did marry her fiancé, whose name was William, and outlived both of her sisters. In fact Doris is still living in the same apartment. She returned to live there when William died three years ago. Doris is fifty-eight now. Marie? She fully recovered from the tragic death of Peter to become an internationally renowned soprano singer of *Lieder*, although she would never forget witnessing the accident that took the life of her former boyfriend. Marie married a music professor who is speaking to you now. She died very young—four years before her sister Frieda at age forty-two—in a car accident."

The young widow, remembering the name of the older gentleman with the thick glasses to be Malcolm Alberts, in connection with Doris's broken arm and the accidental death of Peter with the taxicab, asked if there were any relation between him and Fionn Alberts. Here the professor paused and replied,

"Ah—yes. Malcolm Alberts. He was a distant cousin of Fionn's ex-husband Keith Alberts. He still lives, now aged ninety-two, in a retirement home for the blind."

On hearing this latter revelation, the small gathering fully came to, stirring from their cozy mesmerized state, their eyes and ears returned to the world around them. Overhead the Moon shown full and bright. Several seagulls flew nearby. An entire flock of them had gathered around the group squawking, eager to eat the crumbs left from the sandwiches and pastries.

The party had been wholly oblivious to their surroundings throughout the professor's tale like the childhood-reverted Marie had been in the car next to her cousin Fionn twenty-eight years before. Now they covered the embers that had been the bonfire with sand, gathered their things together, and headed back to their homes. It was after midnight.

Los Angeles
March 24-25
April 2, 2007
July 1, 2013

Jonathan and Anastasia

He sang with an air of disgust and delight. He was a worm who was tired of his disgusting diet of compost and fertilizer, but he knew deep down he was a big bright, beautiful Emperor butterfly who delighted in alighting on small blossoms in the springtime. That was the main reason why he sang *voix céleste* and in *voce di petto*, with such virago and *vibrato*.

He was, after all, a famous tenor operatic star who had sung on every major stage in the world, including at the Met in New York City. No, Jonathan was no ordinary worm. *He* had connections with the theatre and all the big orchestras. *He* had frequented the great opera houses in Stockholm, Copenhagen, and Berlin as a child and youth.

Jonathan was extraordinary, and he knew it, too. Each time he opened his mealy little mouth his throat trembled and overflowed with the most exhilarating song that filled even the largest hall.

True, no one could see him from a distance of more than three yards because of his diminutive person, but what he lacked in size, Jonathan more than made up for in vanity and with his reliable *tour-de-force* performances. No tenor in the history of opera had ever surpassed him in vainglory and attitude. In short, Jonathan was an intelligent but very pompous little earthworm.

Then, one magical evening in the autumn, a sultry snail, who happened to be singing the soprano role of Desdemona in a production of Verdi's *Othello* staged that season at the Civic Opera House in Chicago, managed to win Jonathan's infinitesimal heart. Indeed before this pivotal moment in his life, neither Jonathan nor anyone else even knew he had a heart at all. Nonetheless, Jonathan could not for the life

Reprinted with permission from Alan Lindgren, *Kings & Commoners, Mouse, Magic and More* (Culver City: 2011, Sun Sings Publications), 223–227.

of him find his voice at that moment, because he found himself strangely in love.

Perhaps, we can say today in retrospect, there is a romantic hidden in every worm. Or perhaps it was only the lovely form of her snail shell, which so captivated Jonathan, but Anastasia was no ordinary garden snail either, this much can be said.

Unlike the puffed up Jonathan, young Anastasia was actually rather shy by nature. She slugged her way forward slowly and gracefully, whereas Jonathan inched himself hurriedly and awkwardly across the stage.

Anastasia was the most attractive snail he had ever seen, and she smelled of garden greenery on a summer's afternoon, even though it was a late autumn evening in a musty opera house filled with stodgy sophisticates and other stuffed shirts, which is to say insects and creepy crawly things and flies and whatnot.

You see, Jonathan and Anastasia were famous among garden bugs and beetles, and they sang for earthworms and slugs like themselves, but also for pill bugs and millipedes and centipedes, and even a gnat here and there.

They were a motley crew, and the audiences which Jonathan and Anastasia and their fellow singers drew paid tenderly for admission— tender spinach leaves, Brussels sprouts, baby lettuce, chives, parsley, snow peas, and nasturtiums; and even an occasional carrot top or wild strawberry—whatever they could afford. But only the well-to-do, such as the fireflies and moths, could sit in the balcony, because such pests as cockroaches and houseflies were too cheap and filthy to dress appropriately.

Yes, bugs can and do dress for the opera. There is nothing so gorgeous as a bumblebee in plush velvet, or a queen ant wearing pearls and precious gems. Such guests always sat in the first row.

It was the costumes of the singers that truly took the prize for elegance and extravagance. On this night Jonathan as Othello wore a smart black satin tuxedo with a pink silk bowtie over a frilled purple dress shirt, with a tail cufflink made of diamonds.

But it was Anastasia as Desdemona who out-dazzled them all. She wore nothing but dewdrops on her snail shell, drops which caught the footlights and sparkled like bright stars in every direction to the wonder and amazement of every bug in the house.

You see Anastasia was so beautiful she did not need fancy attire or costly jewelry. Her spiral shell was enough to allure the most selective male grub, and she wore her rounded shell home with poise and demure self-assurance. Anastasia was the darling of the evening, and she stole my heart, too.

She had every insect in the house begging for encore after encore. Even Jonathan temporarily forgot how great he believed he was crawling next to her, because his insides went all soft and mushy each time Anastasia turned in his direction. Anastasia was most definitely the most becoming snail ever to have graced the stage. She was, in one word, charming.

After the performance had ended, and the curtains had come down for the final time, and after the droves of bugs had exited the great opera house, Jonathan found himself alone with Anastasia backstage. The proud worm managed to clear his throat in an almost modest way that betrayed affection, and asked the comely snail if she would care to go out with him to a famous local Spanish beetle nightclub for a drink or two of Tequila (without the worm of course). Anastasia replied she was feeling a bit tired from the evening's exertions, but might Jonathan accompany her to her five-shell snail hotel instead. He was welcome to drink some rainwater she had collected that morning, or munch on a leaf of fresh lettuce from the nursery in her private suite, she said.

Jonathan was of course thrilled by her offer. He readily said he would go with her by bug cab to her hotel, but all he wanted was some rich soil to ingest. Might she have a potted plant somewhere in her room? Anastasia thought that would be lovely, and soon the two singers were cuddled up together on the flowerbed in her suite listening to the sound of rain as it had begun to drizzle and tap on the windowpanes.

When Jonathan awoke it was already ten o'clock on the following morning, and Anastasia was inside of her shell breathing like a little snail angel. Jonathan kissed her lightly and inched his way to the window box to fertilize the soil with the earth he had digested overnight. Then he hailed a bug cab and went to his five-humus worm hotel on the other side of town, but not before leaving Anastasia a little love-note on a grapevine leaf he found on the footpath by the flowerbed.

"Dear Anastasia," the note read. "Thank you for having me over last night. It was a pleasure to be with you, and I hope we can do it again soon. You are truly the most exquisitely beautiful snail I have ever seen, and now I may say spent the night with. Sincerely, Jonathan Worm."

When Anastasia awoke at eleven-thirty later that morning, she found Jonathan's thoughtful message on the grapevine leaf and she smiled, recalling their time together.

"That Jonathan! He's such a sweet worm. He may be a bit arrogant on stage, but deep inside he is a gentle and unassuming grub."

Meanwhile Jonathan felt happier than he had ever felt in his entire life. He whistled to himself all the way back to his hotel and was already making plans for a date with Anastasia at the Insect Theatre in San Francisco as he had connections there.

But this was never to be. Later that same day, at about four-thirty in the afternoon, when Anastasia was slowly slugging her way across the sidewalk to get into a bug cab (she had to be at the Chicago Honeybee Airport in an hour to catch the six o'clock flight to San Francisco), a tall businessman wearing alligator shoes stepped on her, squishing her beyond recognition. Soon the insect paramedics had arrived, but nothing could be done to save her. Young Anastasia had died instantaneously, leaving but a broken shell, and when Jonathan learned of her tragic death, his little heart broke, too.

Jonathan lost his great tenor voice and never sang again. He died several years later in a garden for the worm blind in Memphis, Tennessee. He was penniless, destitute, and lost at the time of his death. He and Anastasia went down in insect history as the unlikeliest operatic lovers of all time.

To this day there is a small plaque in the Chicago Arboretum where Jonathan Worm and Anastasia Snail are immortalized. Each year bugs of all kinds creep, crawl, and fly from across the globe to the Arboretum to pay a visit in their honor.

Los Angeles
June 9, 2007

Johnson's New Friend

The weather was unusual, to say the least. Although a storm appeared to be brewing directly overhead, the sun beamed mightily to the east. It was a strange morning in the early summer.

Johnson was out walking. He was always out walking. Rain or shine, Johnson walked. And walked. On this weird morning in early July, Johnson took the time to dig down into his left pocket. He recalled having put a coin there on the previous night. He fished it out. There it was, a beautiful lustrous gold Liberty dollar. He put it back into his pocket where it was safe and secret.

Johnson sat down on a large rock before the entrance to the forest. He took off his knapsack, putting it on his knees, and pulled out the sack lunch his dear Mother had prepared for him that morning. In it he discovered an orange, a can of apple juice, a roast beef sandwich with horseradish, mayonnaise, and tomato, and a piece of chocolate cake. He paused, wondering where he should begin.

Three hours later, Johnson was deep in the forest when it began to rain. He removed his raincoat, rain hat, and umbrella from the bottom of his knapsack, and readied himself for a downpour, because he had seen and sensed the storm brewing. Above him, the heavens thundered, and the rain poured down in sheets, drenching the trees, the ferns, the mosses, and all the forest life.

Johnson looked for shelter, but found none. He wandered for a while and then saw the opening of a cave about fifteen yards ahead of him. Soon Johnson found himself far inside the cave, and he could hear the rain showering down and saw occasional flashes of lightning lighting up the cave like electric shocks. Then he heard a sound like a

Reprinted with permission from Alan Lindgren, *Kings & Commoners, Mouse, Magic and More* (Culver City: 2011, Sun Sings Publications), 229–231.

moaning coming from behind a rock no more than five feet from his left foot.

"Hello?" he said. "Hello? Are you alright?"

Again, the air trembled lightly with the groaning. Johnson was moved. Something stirred within his heart, a mixture of tenderness, compassion, and love. He walked over to the rock and looked over it to the other side. There lay a small dog that whimpered when it saw him. At once Johnson realized the poor thing had been injured.

He went closer. The dog showed no fear or anger. It only cried out softly, as if for help. Johnson leaned over and touched it. The dog moaned deeply again. Johnson saw blood on his hand, and then on the dog's belly. It had been shot, apparently by a hunter, and had managed to wander into the cave where it finally lay down out of weariness and misery.

But it was not dying. The bullet had pierced its skin, ripping a hole in its side, but the wound was not deep. It was pain that kept the dog lying there, contorting its body from sheer agony.

Johnson removed his raincoat, and then a scarf he had been wearing. He walked out to the cave's entrance and soaked the scarf in rainwater that had collected in a hollowed-out stone. Then he returned to the inner recesses of the cave and the little dog, and applied the water-soaked scarf to its belly, wiping the blood away slowly and as gently as possible so that he could see the wound. The dog groaned loudly.

"There, there, little one. Soon you will feel much better."

Then Johnson noticed a hole in the dog's tummy filled with dark blood whence the liquid had been oozing. He took out his pocketknife and opened it, carefully probing inside the hole. Again the dog did not move or growl, but only cried out more loudly.

There was the bullet. Johnson removed it. It was large and shiny and looked like it was made of silver. He placed the bullet on his raincoat and applied the wet scarf to the affected area.

Over the next several hours, Johnson lovingly nursed the injured dog. It responded at once, licking his hand over and over again. Gradually, it gained in strength. Johnson picked up the little thing into his arms and carried it to the cave's opening. Outside the rain had stopped coming down, and all was fresh and new. He found a small pool of water and put the dog down next to it. Immediately it began to drink, lapping up the water thirstily.

Johnson found himself more and more attached to his new friend. He found there was room for the dog in his knapsack with its body inside and its head peeking out from the top. He marched out of the forest and made his way across the field that led to his home. There his Mother was waiting for his return. When she saw the small happy dog looking out from the top of Johnson's knapsack in curiosity, she remarked,

"I see you've found yourself a friend. Bring the young thing into the house. I'll put out a bowl of milk for him, and a soup bone, too."

Johnson took off his knapsack and quietly picked up the small dog, placing it on the floor. Soon it found its legs and was eagerly lapping up the milk. Johnson reached into his left pocket and felt the coin, his gold Liberty dollar.

"I am very lucky today," he thought to himself. "I've made a new friend."

Los Angeles
June 29-30, 2007
July 1, 2013

Stevenson and the Books

The room was quiet when Stevenson entered at eight-thirty that evening. He turned on the lamp, hung his coat in the closet, and put his wallet and keys on the dresser by his bed next to his alarm clock. Next Stevenson selected a volume of his favorite poems from the book cabinet, which stood in the corner of the room, sat down in his armchair, opened the book to a random page, and began reading aloud:

> The sparrows small love little things
> Beyond the palaces of kings
> Where humble peasants work the earth
> Near Bethlehem of Saviour's birth
>
> They sing their songs of sorrow's ode
> The Child, the Christ must walk His Road
> He who comforts little birds
> In midwinter Mary's words
>
> Are plain and simple in the night
> Beneath the Moon and starry light
> She is Queen of faerie way
> She holds small Jesu faerie lay
>
> Within the manger quietly
> And rocks the baby tenderly
> Against her breast she warms His nose
> He who is the heavenly Rose

Reprinted with permission from Alan Lindgren, *Kings & Commoners, Mouse, Magic and More* (Culver City: 2011, Sun Sings Publications), 233–236.

He who must encounter death
He who taking human breath
Must suffer scorn's disdain of men
The pain of thorns upon His head

But now Jesu Christ is Child
With His Mother Mary mild
All is stillness in this place
The sweetest smile on His face.

Stevenson lay the book down on the small table to his left after closing it with a bookmark where he had just read. The bookmark was given him by an old friend, a gentleman in Ireland fifty years before to the day when he was visiting his Mother in the outskirts of Dublin. On the bookmark were the words, handwritten in ink in calligraphy and still quite legible: *Jesu, tender little boy. How I love thee, sweetest joy. Tools of wood thy only toy. Future cross foretold employ.*

Now Stevenson stood up and exchanged the book for another volume from the same cabinet. It was a novel by a minor French writer of the 18th century translated into English. The book was printed in 1910 and was worn with time and use. It was bound in leather and bore the title *The Kingdom of Childhood*: *A Tale of Magic and Friendship.* The writer was quite unknown to history, a man by the name of Sainte Antoine Jean-Pierre d'Allemagne. Stevenson sat back down in the armchair and opened the book where another bookmark had been inserted. He read, this time in silence:

"Artemis loved to play in the garden of his aunt who lived in the neighboring village in an old house made of stone and wood.

"The garden was large and wonderful. Populated by elemental beings with whom Artemis played (quite unknown to his aunt), a great oak grew in the middle surrounded by uncultivated grass and interesting weeds. Artemis placed blocks of orange brick all around the oak, and outside his fortress little daisies and dandelions delighted in the daylight along with the other weeds in the grass.

"Sparrows lived in the branches of the oak and filled the summer air with joyous song. They often flew down to the grass among the daisies and the dandelions to find breadcrumbs Artemis's aunt put out for them every morning after breakfast. Artemis liked to lie down on his back on the grass and watch the sparrows hop about pecking the crumbs, then fly back up to their home in the branches.

"There was a small wall all around the garden about waist-high of a man. Wild roses grew up over the wall from outside into the garden filling the warm air with the sweetest aromatic fragrance. Honeybees buzzed about the wild roses everywhere and flew down to visit the dandelion and daisy blossoms to drink their nectars. The wild roses were mostly red and white, with an occasional yellow one interspersed here and there.

"The mood in the garden during the summers when Artemis visited his aunt was always gladsome and heartwarming.

"A small well was against the wall just outside the garden, and Artemis liked to draw up water in little buckets and pour it over the ground inside his brick fortress. Then he would mix the water with the earth with a stick and form sculptures made of the mud with his hands.

"Artemis came to stay with his aunt each summer from the time he was three years old until he left France for America at the age of eleven. In America he stayed in a boarding house in a small town in upstate New York for two years before moving out to California to live with his parents in Santa Cruz in a large house with a swimming pool.

"But Artemis never forgot the summers with his aunt and the magic garden where he had played."

Stevenson put the bookmark where he had stopped reading, closed the novel, went back to the cabinet, and exchanged it for a third book. This was an atlas of Africa. After making himself comfortable in the armchair, he opened the atlas to Tunisia and began studying maps of this small country on the Mediterranean Sea across from Italy.

Stevenson recited the names of places, towns, and villages aloud: *Bizerte, Carnoi, Carthage, Cape Bon, Djerba, Hammamet, Matmata, Monastir, Nabeul, Sfax, Sidi Bou Saïd, Sousse, Tabarka.* He decided he would visit these places some day.

At midnight the alarm sounded. Stevenson stirred, having fallen asleep, felt with his hand in the direction of the dresser, located the clock by touch, and turned off the alarm. He got ready for bed, turned off the lamp, and soon he was sound asleep, dreaming about Tunisia, Artemis, and Bethlehem. It was Christmas night.

Los Angeles
February 19-20, 2009

Man and Baby

Cached between my socks and two bars of DIAL® soap, I found a petunia my wife had put into my suitcase. Although I'm not particularly a petunia-lover, I do like flowers—all kinds—and my wife knows this. So this small discovery brought a warm smile to my lips, which is to say to my heart, because my lips are a direct expression of my heart.

Then I heard a rattling. I had a window seat on the bus, taking the Greyhound north from Los Angeles to San Jose. The other seat was unoccupied. I wiped the window with my hand a few times as it was fogged over, and peered out in an attempt to find the source of the rattling.

Then I noticed a movement between my legs, which I felt at the same time. There was a baby—about twelve months old—crawling between my ankles and shaking a small rattle in its left hand. I looked around to see if I could locate its Mother or father, but everyone was seated quietly, either asleep or reading. So I bent over and picked up the baby, who apparently took a liking to me. I say this because it was all smiles and giggles as I propped it up on my lap and smiled right back.

Now I have always liked babies. I did some real babysitting (not just with older children) back in my college days and took pride that I could change a mean diaper. My wife and I wanted to have our own child, but we hadn't had any luck yet. So this little one was doing a pretty good job filling in for my own—at least until it was reunited with its Mom or Dad.

Soon I was engrossed in playing peek-a-boo, a game which

Reprinted with permission from Alan Lindgren, *Kings & Commoners, Mouse, Magic and More* (Culver City: 2011, Sun Sings Publications), 243–245.

delights most any small child, and frankly I enjoy peek-a-boo as much as do these little ones. We went on like this for about five minutes until it wanted to explore, and if you've ever got a baby who wants to crawl around but isn't allowed to—even if it's for a perfectly valid reason (like it's not safe on the aisle of a moving bus packed with passengers)—well then you know what a job you've got on your hands.

Babies don't just accommodate themselves to practical necessities. They have insistent little wills of their own. So what may be inarguably necessary in the eyes of an adult can be diametrically opposite to the very real demands of the tiny one under your care. And, tiny or not, a baby is nothing ignorable, unless it's sleeping quietly in its crib or is being fed at its Mother's breast (so long as you're not the Mother), so I found myself in a tight situation.

I decided to try one tactic that worked for a while. I bounced the baby up and down on my knees while making funny faces. Let me assure you, children *do* appreciate funny faces. It's the adults and high school kids who are too old for such immature things.

Who needs maturity, anyway? I may not be a spring chicken, but I still *feel* young. Well, this little guy really did enjoy my antics, and soon we were both having a ball of fun. Only after a few minutes, my arms began to tire. I guess I don't work out enough. Or else writing uses different muscles. At any rate, it was time to try something else.

Fortunately for me, this time my little friend figured out our next move when it reached out with its free hand (it was still clutching its rattle in its left hand) and slapped its open palm against the glass window, the very same one I had looked out of when all of this began. Instead of pulling it away, wisely (pat on the back), I scooted closer to the window and watched to see what would happen next.

Would you believe it: The child pressed its nose (and entire face, because babies' noses are very small and cartilaginous) against the glass surface, then pulled back again, absolutely thrilled! Back-and-forth, back-and-forth, this exciting new game went on for at least ten more minutes.

Then I felt a squeeze on my upper arm. When I turned, a nice man was looking down at me from the aisle with a big grin on his good face.

"Thanks for taking care of my baby," he said warmly. "I dozed off, and Joey is very good at getting around."

Sadly, I handed Joey over to his father, for I had grown very attached to this extremely active little child.

"O, Joey's a good boy," I smiled back with sincerity. "Just let me know if you need another nap. I babysat in my youth," I added braggingly.

Los Angeles
October 7-8, 2009

146

Martha

"Ferdinand! Ferdinand!"

A mother called out loud. She was looking, not for her husband, not for her poodle (for she had neither), but for her only child, her son of ten years.

Ferdinand had lost his father, a thief and a drunk, to an auto wreck at age four. His Mother, a slight and frail but comely woman by the name of Martha, earned her living sewing and stitching the clothing of wealthy women and men who paid her little for her excellent work.

Martha was simple. Not simple-minded, rather plain and ordinary, like a naive girl who looks at life and sees nothing complex in it but only poor and rich, hardworking and easy-living, weak and strong, sickly and healthy, weary and refreshed, ill-fortuned and lucky. She belonged to the former group, and although she would have gladly exchanged her station in life with someone on the upscale, Martha accepted her lot without question or hope.

She was neat and tidy, and she kept the small flat where she lived with her son clean and friendly, though she owned nothing special or posh with which to decorate it. Simple linen adorned the simple furniture; a table, a few chairs, two beds, a bedside table (all very modest). The walls were painted a cheery yellow that contrasted nicely with the light blue and pale purple rugs on the wood floor.

Each morning Martha made breakfast (hot cereal, toast with jam, and juice, and Sundays one hardboiled egg for each), put on a fresh tablecloth and set the table for two, called Ferdinand to come, and she

Reprinted with permission from Alan Lindgren, *Kings & Commoners, Mouse, Magic and More* (Culver City: 2011, Sun Sings Publications), 279–293.

and her son sat down and ate, Ferdinand in silence, Martha talking about little things that were of concern to her, or of no import, but always in her light and friendly manner.

Ferdinand was a lonely boy who always managed to fill his pockets with knickknacks—pieces of metal, old keys, watch chains, cheap broken jewelry, dirty coins, discarded things—and whose only friends were the empty streets at dusk, the dusty attic where he sat for hours weekends and arranged his knickknacks, the weeds that grew in empty lots, and soft bird feathers that he carefully collected and put under his bed with his other prized possessions: a pine cone, a miniature school bus, a match box containing fifteen good wood matches, and a pack of cigarettes that he never smoked.

After breakfast Martha gave her son the sack lunch she had prepared for him that consisted in a tuna sandwich, an apple, a small orange juice, and two oatmeal cookies, and kissed his forehead. Ferdinand sadly left, for he did not like school.

School meant the mean children who made fun of him, the boring classes with the lady instructors who wore too much makeup and perfume, and looked over the children's shoulders to ensure they took down every word they said, the uncomfortable chairs and outdated school desks, the chalkboards he and the other children had to write the solutions to math problems on, the asphalt school grounds where he sat on an old metal bench during recess while the other boys played rugby and the girls talked amongst themselves—Ferdinand did not like school.

After Ferdinand had left for school, Martha dusted and swept and mopped the apartment, ironed the bed linen, and did up the few dishes. Then she began to mend her clients' clothes that she picked up from the other side of town each weekday at three o'clock in the afternoon after dropping off the clothes she had mended and received her pay. This was half a schilling for a coat or a dress, fifteen pence for a pair of trousers or a skirt, five pence for a shirt, and tuppence for a pair of socks.

The work was tedious and taxing, and Martha often stayed up until midnight to meet her schedule, only to rise again at half past five the next morning to begin another day of hard work. But it was preferable to the hazardous labor in the dark grungy factories and especially to life in the squalor of the slums, where only running errands for thruppence or prostitution were the means to scrape by.

Martha often worried about Ferdinand, who was such a taciturn boy. She wished he would talk to her and share his concerns so that she could comfort him with kind words and affection, but he was an introverted child who kept to himself. Martha tried to make his days brighter, and she kept his poor clothes in good condition using quality fabrics left over from her clients' throwaways to mend them, something which only made a ridiculous-looking spectacle out of Ferdinand that brought laughter from his schoolmates and the girls especially who could be so merciless.

But Ferdinand bore all this heartless teasing as though it were only natural. He accepted it along with all of the other unpleasant aspects of school as a given and only shrugged his shoulders when a particularly cruel boy or girl taunted him in front of all the others, pushing him or spitting on him. He came to be so used to this mistreatment that it was an expected part of his days at school.

His true happiness lay hidden in the attic and under his bed, where his imagination had full reign, and his inner life found its secret joys. There, he was left alone. There, no other child could reach him. There, no trouble with his teachers was to be found. There, he was special.

As to Martha, Ferdinand did love his Mother. But owing to his reticence, and his inability to see and therewith take an interest in his surroundings, which included people, he had no way to express this love and the tenderness that touched his young heart because he knew how hard his Mother worked, what a hard life she led, how hard it was for her to be a widow, her feelings about their poverty, all of which regarding himself he accepted and did not really mind.

Towards himself Ferdinand was actually quite aloof, and no one could injure his dignity, not even the meanest slights of his peers or the complete want of respect in his physical environment. No, the dignity of Ferdinand was entirely independent of all external support, so he required no special treatment by anyone or outer trappings to serve a need that someone who depends on good fortune finds a necessity. His esteem reposed in himself and therein alone. So he was content with his lonely existence, although secretly he longed to confide in someone his inmost thoughts and sentiments.

Martha, on the other hand, was equally sociable to his reclusion. She chatted with her clients and their servants good-naturedly, just as she was always ready to visit with the shopkeeper at the market and with the other women who made their purchases there. For this reason she was well-liked and even popular, for she was naturally friendly and liked to cheer people up, not due to her own humble circumstances and misfortune, but only because that was her human nature.

When, on preparing to return home after picking up a load of work from one of her rich clients one day (it was a Friday), a handsome gentleman offered to accompany her to her flat, Martha was agreeable.

Soon she was engaging the man in a light discussion on this and that as though her life were as sunny as her apartment walls were yellow. When they arrived Martha invited the gentleman in, completely oblivious to the fact that she had nothing to offer him but her merry company and a cup of tea in an old teacup, which was so nice that he readily accepted.

Ferdinand was outside collecting knickknacks at the time, while Martha made peppermint tea that she poured and served with a small plate of her oatmeal cookies—three cookies to be exact.

"Mr. Daniels,"

Martha remarked, for that was the gentleman's name, as he took a bite of a cookie he had placed on the table next to his teacup,

"You are such a nice chap. You hardly see a better-dressed man. Who mends your clothes?"

"O, I take them to the tailor when they require tending," replied Mr. Daniels.

"Why, I could do the job for you for one-third the price. That's what I do—sew and stitch clothes. And a fine job, I might add. I see the hem of your trousers could use some taking in. I'd charge you fifteen pennies—that's all."

"Mrs. Marks," the gentleman retorted. "I wouldn't pay you less than five shillings. You really should charge your clients more. Your simple dress is impeccable. You would look pretty in an evening gown. Perhaps you would allow me to buy you one, and we might go out to a show one night."

"O, but I have my work to do—and a son to look after."

"You have a son. How old is the boy?"

"Ten last month. Ferdinand is very quiet, but a good lad. He just needs his Mother's care, if only I had more I could give him!"

Here Martha began to weep, for the thought of her hard life and sad son temporarily broke her joy.

"There, there, Mrs. Marks,"

Mr. Daniels patted her on the shoulder gently.

"Take my handkerchief. I'm sure Ferdinand couldn't have a better mother. And I know he wouldn't mind if I took you to a show twice a week. I will reimburse you for your time, mind you, because you'll lose some work-money. But you will enjoy getting out in the company of a gentleman. Am I right?" he stated rather than asked.

"O! Mr. Daniels! What should I say!?! I say yes! Why, I'd like that. Really I would!"

"Good. Now tomorrow afternoon I'll come by at three-thirty to do some shopping. You can pick out a nice dress for an hundred pounds sterling, a hat for twenty, and a pair of pretty shoes for thirty. I'll bring you an attractive necklace and earrings to match. Ferdinand will dine with my servants (they'll feed him an excellent meal), and we will eat out at my favorite restaurant. After an eight-course dinner at Benson's, my chauffeur will drive us cross-town to Fifth and Helmsley in one of the Rolls. There's a beautiful theatre there, and this weekend *Alexander and Fedora* is on stage. The actors are the best, and I will astonish my friends with my lovely female companion."

"Mr. Daniels! Well..., well..., I'll tell Ferdinand when he comes home. O, Mr. Daniels! I'm so happy! Now, let me take in your hem. Just bring these trousers tomorrow when you come by to take little Martha out. I'll have them ready for pick-up by three o'clock Sunday, ready to wear."

"For ten quid, no less. You must accept. It's not much, but it's the least I can do."

And so began the flirtation and dating of Martha Marks and Mr. James Daniels.

****

When Martha told Ferdinand about James Daniels and her date at the dinner table that evening, he said nothing, showing no interest. When she said he would be eating really good food with Mr. Daniels's servants, Ferdinand also expressed inattention, saying nothing.

But he was curious. He wanted to see what he would be eating, to taste it to see if he liked it, and to eat it, but more than this he wanted to know who this Mr. Daniels was.

Without displaying the slightest emotion, Ferdinand dully mumbled a few words about where Mr. Daniels came from, and what he wanted with his Mother. Understanding his protectiveness, Martha said Mr. Daniels was a fine gentleman she had met coming home from Mrs. Stanley's mansion on Fenton Place in Ipswich. She said he was very nice and that he treated her like a lady. She was sure he would like Mr. Daniels when they met on the next day (Saturday) and that Mr. Daniels was a very fine gentleman.

When Ferdinand said she had already said that, and did she know whether Mr. Daniels were married, Martha was very surprised, that Ferdinand was so talkative and interested both, as he had never demonstrated such abilities before.

Martha replied that Mr. Daniels must be a bachelor who simply took a shine to her, and was that really so surprising, poor as they were?

Ferdinand merely shrugged his shoulders and mumbled, offhandedly, that rich gentlemen keep company with rich people and only employ poor people, as though this were a given and a law.

Martha was now astonished, for Ferdinand stood his ground with quiet strength and unbending resolution, so she said (to settle the matter) that Mr. Daniels knew an honest lady when he saw one, that he liked her company, which is only natural as she was a friendly person and a good hostess, and that she liked Mr. Daniels, too. With that Martha said, and with no little conviction, she had work to do at her sewing, because she had bills to pay and food to put on the table, and she walked out of the kitchen (that doubled as a dining room).

This was the first time Mother and son had ever had a discussion of any substance, and that Martha had had to put her foot down. Ferdinand did not mind his Mother's self-assertion. On the contrary, he respected her for it, and even lingered thoughtfully over his potatoes and peas before going up to the attic to play. That is the way Mr. James Daniels entered the life of Ferdinand Marks, and there was nothing that could alter this one iota.

****

James Daniels was a widower four times when he met Martha Marks. He had been a clerk in a newspaper office when he frequented social events and made appearances at art shows to make a name for himself as a popular bachelor. He met Betty at a club; the wealthy woman was taken by his good looks, boyish charm, and worldly ways. Betty died of pleurisy, leaving Mr. Daniels with two million quid and a daughter.

His second wife was Agatha. Agatha was anemic. She died one month to the day after their extravagant Wedding. Agatha left James Daniels with her entire fortune, which consisted in a large estate in the country, seventeen indentured servants, a collection of ladies' jewelry valued at eight million pounds sterling, and a stable with seven thoroughbred horses.

His third wife Joan was the daughter of an earl and a heavy drinker who died at the age of twenty-two of cirrhosis of the liver. Joan left James with fifteen million pounds sterling.

His fourth wife was Pauline. Pauline was his most beautiful wife. She was also suicidal and had been since her Mother had died in an airplane crash when she was eight years old. Pauline was constantly depressed and slept little, and she was addicted to various 'medicinal substances'. She died of an overdose of sleeping pills at age twenty-five, leaving James with five million quid, the mansion where they had lived for three years, one limousine, three Rolls Royce, two Bentleys, and a staff of servants; including a chauffeur, a butler, a cook, and three maids. James was living there at the time he began courting Martha.

James Daniels did not want for property, servants, or money.

****

After their first date Martha was as intoxicated. She drank only one glass of expensive red wine, but it wasn't the alcohol that had this effect. She had never dined out, let alone at such a famous and elegant restaurant, or been to a play.

The meal alone cost Mr. Daniels two hundred pounds sterling. They had box seats at the theatre—the best in the house—and Martha was as beautiful in her new outfit and jewelry as the prettiest girl there. She verily shone with her powdered pale white skin against a gown of pink taffeta and matching hat and shoes, and adorned in the fine silver necklace and sparkling silver emerald earrings James had given her.

James Daniels had caught a lovely little lady, and every one was talking about her, just who was this Martha Marks they had never laid eyes on before. He only said a mutual friend had introduced them, which was partially true as Mrs. Stanley, under whose employ Martha was, was his acquaintance, and he was just taking leave of her when Martha had stopped by with Mrs. Stanley's newly mended clothes to be recompensed and to pick up the next allotment.

James Daniels loved leading the life of the very wealthy, but he was tired of the falsity under whose pretenses his four wives had lived and married him. He had no qualms with his own pretensions and falsehood, but he was most attracted to the unassuming Martha, who took such delight in what the rest of the company only flaunted. It was precisely Martha's simplicity and spontaneous joy that gave her a special charm, and as James Daniels had no need for more money, he could devote his attentions to poor Martha and her childlike demeanor.

Inexperienced Martha was completely unaware of all this. She adored Mr. Daniels because he was taken by her, and she was excited by all the phony glitter that surrounded the well-to-do, because it was all so costly and new to her, so seemingly beautiful, and because of its great appeal to her nature.

Martha

What she had previously jealously wished for that had been far out-of-reach, Martha had now sampled, and it was very much to her liking. She was so happy that, were it not for her maternal instincts, Martha wouldn't have noticed Ferdinand's moping, that he did not like the change he saw in his Mother, and that he only distanced himself further into his own world.

****

"Ferdinand,"

Martha asked her son over breakfast that first Monday.

"How was the dinner at the mansion on Saturday?"

Ferdinand only played with his porridge, saying nothing.

"Mr. Daniels said his servants liked you, and that every one thinks you're a good lad."

Again. No comment.

"You seem so unhappy, Ferdinand. Why don't you tell your Mother about it? I can't help you if I don't know why."

Ferdinand took a few spoonfuls of his porridge, swallowed some of his apple juice, grabbed his toast and jam, didn't touch the slice of lemon cake his Mother had baked especially for him, and stood up.

"You're not eating your breakfast, Ferdinand. Here. Here is your lunch. I made you a ham sandwich this morning. Maybe it will make you feel better."

Ferdinand took his sack lunch and dejectedly left the flat after his Mother had kissed him lovingly on the forehead.

Martha didn't know what to do. As she dusted, swept, and mopped the small rooms of the flat, she tried to think of some way to reach her son, but her thoughts kept turning to her wonderful evening with Mr. Daniels.

She walked to her closet and took out her new dress and hat. She breathed the perfume from the bottle Mr. Daniels had bought for her. This reminded her of the earrings, so she went over to her little bedside table and took them out. She put on the earrings, and then the necklace. Then she admired herself in the broken mirror in the little bathroom. Soon she had forgotten all about Ferdinand's sudden withdrawal.

This repeated itself each day of the week. Then came the weekend with more dining out, and theatre—and dancing, and Martha was caught up in a whirlwind of wine, laughter, parties, perfume, and high society. Several weeks went by like this, frequently with a new dress or shoes, sometimes a new hat or perfume, and always flowers, white roses, pink roses, red roses.

Ferdinand invariably went grumpily to James Daniels's mansion to dine with the servants while his Mother was out for the evening. Although he did like the food (that far exceeded any cooking Martha could prepare with her modest means), he remained distrustful of Mr. Daniels and never once revealed to his Mother his inner thoughts and feelings. Sometimes the three of them drove out to Mr. Daniels's estate in the countryside where Ferdinand spent long hours in the stables with the horses. But he spoke not a word to his host, and only mumbled to his Mother that he wanted to return to the apartment in the city.

Meanwhile Martha had fallen in love under the charms, gallantry, and wealth of James Daniels, of which the man was fully cognizant, and in which he was experienced.

Easily he led her, step-by-step, as an innocent child is led by the hand through a beautiful house filled with wonderful things, into his rich, grand, and captivating world, deceiving her in her naivety as to what was really happening.

Three months, eleven elegant dresses, nineteen pairs of shoes, nine stylish hats, and a pricey lady's wristwatch later, Mr. James Daniels proposed to Martha Marks on the west balcony of his country estate precisely at sunset.

Martha quivered with the thrill of joy and accepted with a "Yes, James! I will marry you and be your wife forever!" Then the man removed a small velvet box from his trousers pocket and opened it, exposing a small, very expensive white gold diamond engagement ring, which he slid onto her finger, finalizing his long-made plans. Ferdinand was hiding behind a tree below the balcony at the time, and he witnessed the whole affair with the greatest suspicion.

James Daniels intended to name Martha in his will on their Wedding night, bequeathing her with half his wealth and holdings just before bedding her, but he was killed by a horse-drawn carriage on his way to pick her up for a sumptuous meal at a particularly pricey restaurant.

Instead his entire fortune went to his only child Madeline, his very spoiled sixteen year-old daughter by his first wife Betty, and Martha was left without a fiancé, and with twelve dresses, twenty pair of shoes, ten stylish hats, several bottles of the finest ladies' perfume, a silver necklace, a pair of silver emerald earrings, a high-priced lady's wristwatch, and a costly white gold diamond engagement ring.

Martha sold the dresses, shoes, and hats but for one outfit and kept the jewelry, returning to her ordinary life of daily toil and drudgery. Ferdinand dropped out of school at age fifteen. He bought a sturdy bicycle with money his Mother gave him and became a courier in London.

To this day poor Martha Marks labors away, meticulously sewing and stitching the clothes of wealthy clients, and she frequently recalls with fondness the spring she was courted by and engaged to James and received his lavish attentions. Then she removes all of her clothes, except for a plain white slip, puts on the dress, shoes, and hat, and all of her costly jewelry, looks at herself in the broken bathroom mirror, and smiles, imagining herself to be the very rich wife of a very, very wealthy gentleman by the name of Mr. James Daniels.

Los Angeles
October 19-21, 2009
Edited November 14/17, 2010
July 2013

Four Brief Prose Sketches for Youth and Adults

Four Scenes

Early One Morning in the City

The Father in Baghdad

The Youthful Stranger

Four Scenes

The Boy

A child, a boy of six years, looked out the window of the airplane from his window seat and saw the clouds below. He had been observing how the plane had been flying higher and higher in elevation, the houses, trees, mountains, and bodies of water on the earth growing smaller and smaller in his view with the increasing distance. He wrote in his diary: "Now we are above the clouds."

The plane later landed at Heathrow International Airport in London. From there he and his family crossed by boat to Denmark where they traveled by train to Copenhagen. The boy drew a picture of a train in his diary. From Copenhagen they took the ferry to Sweden.

Sweden was for him a land of magic and wonder. The family visited his father's relatives on the West Coast near Uddevalla (not far from Gothenburg) where his aunt and uncle had made their home near a fjord in a place called Skäret.

In his memory dwelled the special smell of this home, the image of a large model ship contained in a glass bottle, and outside there was a moss-covered stone-cropping and a little forest with a stone step-path. He and his sister often walked in their new wooden shoes through this forest, his red, hers dark blue, over the stepping stones until they came to the other side upon a big open lawn with a tall flag pole on which the blue and yellow Swedish flag waved high above. This was the front yard belonging to the house of a family where the boy and his sister

Reprinted with permission from Alan Lindgren, *The Courage of the Flame: Ballads, Sonnets and Other Gardens of Poetry with Prose Writings* (Culver City: 2003, Sun Sings Publications), 182–184; and *Kings & Commoners, Mouse, Magic and More* (2011), 301–304.

had come to meet another little boy and girl about their ages who lived there. One sunny afternoon the four children sat at a picnic table on the big lawn celebrating the little girl's birthday with cake and ice cream.

It often rained in Sweden, and the little boy and his sister especially loved to walk through the forest in the falling raindrops and to be in the wide-open spaces in the wet drizzling misty weather. The earth was breathing out her summer warmth, mingling with the moisture coming from the heavens, creating a thick rich atmosphere in the forest.

The stone-cropping was ancient, beautiful large rocks with great rounded surfaces upon which moss and lichen grew. They loved the moisture of this rainy part of the world, and the stone took on a deep bluish hue when wet.

The boy liked to climb on these great bluish rocks with their green mosses, which filled his young heart with excitement and wonder.

It was an enchanted land in which his imagination had full play, and his heart leapt with his feet while the rain brought his thoughts down near the earth among the rocks of the stone-cropping and the moss.

The Young Man

Many years later, now a man in his 20s, he sat again in a window seat of an airplane slowly approaching its destination of Los Angeles. Far below were the mountains. Rivers and lakes sometimes appeared threading and dotting the deep blue-green landscape. As the plane neared Los Angeles it began its descent, and smaller sights such as roads and housing developments could be made out. Greater Los Angeles spread itself out hugely across the basin in its giant sprawl, seemingly limitless.

The homes grew larger, and swimming pools occasionally dotted the scene below. Departing planes flew out over the Pacific, the great ocean vast and blue. His plane was heading for LAX International Airport, and the buildings and streets appeared larger and larger. Soon the plane neared the runway and then touched down with a sudden motion announcing its arrival on solid ground.

The young man joined the stream of passengers walking through the gate toward the luggage area where everyone on his flight gathered. He stood there until his bags came and, picking up the suitcases, he walked out to the curb where his mother was waiting in the car. He was very tired and weary from many days travel.

A flash of memories struck him following the myriad impressions of cars, freeways, gas stations, streetlights, people, and the great jumble the big cities are. He longed for quiet inner places where he could picture scenes and dreams. He closed his eyes and soon fell fast asleep. The following images began to appear.

The Party

Solid men and fluid women danced in a whirl to floating drones of music. On the rack by the door hats of all kinds and sizes and various coats hung in disarray like empty people in a reverie. The host stood grandly orchestrating the serving of champagne to the shuffle of dozens of feet. The dancing broke up and the company began to mingle.

From 8 o'clock it was soon 9, then 10, and by the midnight hour the music picked up and the dancers were back on the floor moving to the pulsing rhythms like the wild flames of a midsummer bonfire. The non-dancing crowd cheered and toasted, sending the dancers into heightened stepping as the music played feverishly.

Hours passed in an eternity of motion until, finally, the drinks finished, the dancers stood still, the music stopped. Quietly, and in an almost shamed hush, coats and hats were put on, and the company went out into the pale of early morning.

Faces

Images of faces appeared everywhere to every one in unexpected places. On the sidewalk, in a crack in the wall, on the dashboard of a car, by the traffic light, in the air straight ahead, people everywhere were seeing images of faces. Faces long forgotten appeared in clarity and began speaking, calling out for remembrance.

People were leaving their cars, left the movie theatres without seeing the shows, left their jobs in the middle of the shift, left the malls, and stood looking at one another whispering of these faces.

Friends who had quarreled or who were out-of-touch were reconciled to one another and spoke intimately, broken families were reunited, strangers and the homeless were taken in. School children, some of whom had never visited an old person, filled the convalescent homes joining the old folk, many of whom had not seen a child in years. There were long and personal conversations, old songs were sung, and in other places people simply gathered in deserted rooms and libraries where they sat listening to the silence or to the birds singing outside.

Those accustomed to not being listened to spoke openly, and those who often talked without having anything to say listened. People were themselves, but not hurried, not rushing about or busy or late for anything. No one had anything to do but to meet and congregate and share in human company.

The faces remained, the faces of departed souls, the faces of the dead, comforting, consoling, bringing joy, speaking tenderly and kindly to everyone. And peace dwelled in human hearts, and all was well.

Early One Morning in the City

Outside in empty lots and earthen places along the sidewalks where weeds grew and flourished, litter lay strewn about. Old newspapers, cardboard cigarette cartons, cigarette butts, napkins, Kleenex®, paper towels, paper bags, Styrofoam and paper cups and plates, gum wrappers, all had carelessly gathered in these forgotten corners of the world like the mentally ill and the homeless who now slept there among rags in the cold of night before the dawn.

This litter, once thoughtlessly discarded like the tired hungry men and women now lying there in sweet dreams of warm doughnut shops and fast food restaurants, appeared changed in taking on a ghostly spirit-white brilliance, blazing brightly like burning magnesium in the night.

And I realized as I walked by these empty lots and places along the sidewalks where the weeds grew, the litter shone, and the homeless slept, that this was the spirit-land of the dead.

The weeds and birds (which now singing to the dawn caught my attention) were spirit-archetypes of their earthly counterparts, the streets and sidewalks spirit-roads and spirit-paths, the mentally ill and the homeless spirits of the dead, the litter discarded memories of time and space pure fresh white in spirit-metamorphosis.

I came to the doughnut shop I sought, entering its welcoming warmth among the living spirits of the dead. There they sat reading the newspaper, drinking coffee, eating freshly baked doughnuts, and conversing genially with childlike smiles and gestures.

I bought an apple fritter, asked for a cup of water and something to write on. The kind lady gave me an empty cigarette carton, and I took my doughnut, water, and the carton and joined a man who sat with a cup of coffee reading the morning paper. As I ate my fritter and drank the water, I began writing this story. The street traffic rushes by and men and women walk by outside. The morning of the new day has arrived. I decide I like this spiritual city, and I know it is good because I have not forgotten the forgotten people, the mentally ill and the homeless, and the thoughtlessly discarded litter.

Reprinted with permission from Alan Lindgren, *The Courage of the Flame: Ballads, Sonnets and Other Gardens of Poetry with Prose Writings* (Culver City: 2003, Sun Sings Publications), 186; and *Kings & Commoners, Mouse, Magic and More* (2011), 307.

The Father in Baghdad

A child, a small girl is badly wounded, her right foot torn from her body, blood soaking her clothes, dripping to the earth. She is being carried by her poor father down a street in an impoverished neighborhood in Baghdad just attacked by bombs and missiles of the U.S. and British Air Forces.

She smiles, relaxed in her father's arms in a gesture of open helplessness. She is serene and trusting in the strength of her father who has always loved and cared for her.

He holds her lean body and does not know where to go. As he walks she closes her eyes and breathes her last breath, a look of sweetness on her small face. She leaves her body and her father to grieve and mourn the loss of his only child. He prepares a crude burial for her body in the rubble of the street. He has nowhere to go and decides he will try to find his wife. He does not know it yet, but she was killed minutes earlier in the same attack.

In a few days every one in this neighborhood will join the girl and her mother from lack of water and food. The U.S. and British troops have blocked all roads into Baghdad preventing emergency assistance from coming in.

Above in the sky a solitary bird flies by singing. The Sun slowly makes her way westwards toward the Earth as it is early evening, the close of another day. Charred bodies lie everywhere. Shells of buildings stand smoking, and burned cars, mere frames, litter the streets like carcasses.

Further down the road where the explosions and flames did not reach, an olive tree motions slightly in the gentle breeze and sunshine. Small weeds showing color have begun to flower in the early spring.

Where the father now walks, death is in the blackness of the ruins and bodies, and in the odor of the smoke. This is the holocaust of Iraq, a poor suffering people whose lives now end in tragic violence and pain.

The Father in Baghdad

The souls of the newly dead have already joined with Christ, Who met and carried them over on their passing. They look down on their remains and the deathly scene below and feel the thoughts of their loved ones still on earth. They comfort those who can in inner stillness send them their loving thoughts and feelings, cleansing their burning eyes with tears of sorrow. They help their souls in grief with Sun of Christ in the spiritual world. They are able to enter into their hearts offering solace within.

The departed little girl and mother are together on the Other Side, now closer than they were in earthly life. They hear the bombing as spiritual thunder shaking the heavens while the newly dead enter one after another. Throughout the attacks they hear the cries of children and the weeping of women and men.

Suddenly they are drawn to the father of the girl, the husband of the mother. He has discovered the body of his wife. He has been praying to Allah for their souls. He weeps, kneeling on the ground.

Now he pictures his wife and daughter as they were just the other day talking quietly together over a simple meal. In memory he can hear their voices, see their smiling faces and gesturing hands. He smiles. He feels peaceful knowing their presence within him. The departed wife is giving him courage and support as she did before her death, but now with the spiritual heart of Christ Whom she is with. His little girl is smiling warmly in her father, bringing a smile to his tired face as she did but an hour earlier on the street, but now she is helping him with the glowing smile of Christ's eyes she tenderly beholds her father with.

He slowly rises to his feet and walks down the street in the direction of the setting Sun.

Reprinted with permission from Alan Lindgren, *The Courage of the Flame: Ballads, Sonnets and Other Gardens of Poetry with Prose Writings* (Culver City: 2003, Sun Sings Publications), 187–188; and *Kings & Commoners, Mouse, Magic and More* (2011), 309–310.

The Youthful Stranger

The air inside the library is fresh and cool, ideal for clear thinking and study. Several people are working at the computers, one lady is making photocopies, others are reading books, magazines, and newspapers, children are talking and being read to, and two men are going over plans for the interior of a building. The one sits at the table with pencil making adjustments, while the other stands and sits alternatively, freely making clear quiet comments directly to the point in an inconspicuous and friendly manner.

He is about forty years old, perhaps a few years older, slender, fairly tall, balding with long straight blonde hair, a high round intelligent forehead, small oval wire-frame glasses and clear sparkling blue eyes. His delicate shoulders are rounded, his posture upright, his legs beautiful and well-proportioned. He is wearing shorts and sneakers, and around one ankle a black nylon bandage, perhaps for a sprain.

He speaks fluent English with some kind of European accent, difficult to place, especially since his words are few and softly spoken, and he laughs merrily from time to time.

His movements are fluid and graceful displaying complete ease and freedom and, at the same time, a mood of open love, quiet self-respect, and assurance surrounds him, creating an open, contented relationship to those around him and to the surrounding space.

He reveals an awareness of everything in his environment, human, spatial, intelligent as he moves freely in a continuous graceful line from one consideration to the next without hesitation or break. He remains equally active inwardly and outwardly when silent as when he is speaking quietly.

His appeal lies in the quiet strong attraction he exerts on his surroundings, a hidden magical quality which brings delight and wonder, while ever drawing one's thoughts to his specific features and subtle expressions.

One does not tire of noticing everything about him, indeed wishing to learn ever more and more from his person and lips, yet his love spreads outward encompassing everything and every one in the vicinity such that one is changed in the process.

His strong will asserts itself from the first quietly but more and more powerfully, and this will is at the same time at peace with the world. Harmony and joy are among his other attributes.

Los Angeles
Late 2002
Early 2003

Reprinted with permission from Alan Lindgren, *The Courage of the Flame: Ballads, Sonnets and Other Gardens of Poetry with Prose Writings* (Culver City: 2003, Sun Sings Publications), 189; and *Kings & Commoners, Mouse, Magic and More* (2011), 311–312.

Two Gem Miniatures for All Ages

The Forest in Sweden

The Peasant

The Forest in Sweden

Although it was summer, deep in the shade of the forest all was cool. I sat down on the soft green moss and carefully laid out my precious shells from the sea. I had been collecting them every summer since I was a little boy. I loved their shapes, their surfaces and colors. I knew that they had been homes to sea-creatures, like the empty snail shell is to the snail.

Again with care, I gathered together the seashells in my special box. Now I began exploring the forest for mushrooms and berries. I knew which were poisonous to avoid and which were edible, and I loved the small blueberries that grew on small low-to-the-ground bushes.

Coming on a whole area filled with blueberries, I took out a sack I had been carrying with me and began picking the sweet berries, working quietly on until the bag was three-quarters full.

Then I went to another part of the forest where I found some kantarellar, orange mushrooms, edible and delicious when sautéed in butter, picked a number of them, put them into the sack with the blueberries, and began my way back out of the forest, walking on the soft plush, green moss.

Los Angeles (?)
1995 (?)

Reprinted with permission from Alan Lindgren, *By the Sunset there's a Door: Poetry, Prose and Essays Celebrating Nature and Humanity* (Culver City: 2002, Sun Sings Publications), 237; and *Kings & Commoners, Mouse, Magic and More* (2011), 319–320.

The Peasant

A long time ago there lived a peasant on a farm. His daily life included the carrying out of many chores. Milking the cows, churning the butter, making cheeses, and feeding the farm animals occupied some of his time. In the spring he was often to be seen out in the fields sowing the grain and planting the vegetables.

But when he had any free time, the man loved to walk along an old earthen road as his ancestors had before him, softly singing sweet tunes to himself, especially at the end of the day. Then he would stop walking and gaze for a long time at the heavens, watching the colors change in the sky at the sunset and the first appearing stars.

After looking at the sparkling stars for a good while, he would slowly turn back and walk down the old road to the farm where a meal of bread and cheese and hot tea awaited him. As the next day he would be rising very early, so he retired early to bed after saying a prayer of thanksgiving. He slept well every night as he worked hard during the day, lying on his bed of straw next to the cows, who kept him warm, even in winter.

Los Angeles
Winter 1994-1995

Alan Lindgren

Reprinted with permission from Alan Lindgren, *By the Sunset there's a Door: Poetry, Prose and Essays Celebrating Nature and Humanity* (Culver City: 2002, Sun Sings Publications), 238; and *Kings & Commoners, Mouse, Magic and More* (2011), 362.

About the Author

Alan Lindgren was born in Encino, California in 1962. He is a poet by vocation, and a gifted fiction and non-fiction writer as well. He has forty-seven books published 1987 and 1997–2013. Of his 1,200 plus poems 900 are published. His tales and stories are published. His five biographies and an autobiography are published. Over 130 of his well over 300 articles and essays have seen publication. He is a playwright with four plays published, and the published librettist to an operetta.

Mr. Lindgren's fiction, articles, and poetry have appeared in *Biodynamics*, a publication of the *Bio-Dynamic Farming and Gardening Association, Inc.*, *The Correspondence*, newsletter of the Central Region of the Anthroposophical Society in America, and Highland Hall Waldorf School's newsletter *Rhythms*. His work has been used in an anthroposophical studies-in-English program and displayed at the Chicago Seminary of the Christian Community and a Christian Community church for students, members, and others.

He is a lyric poet. He has composed poetry since 1986, written fiction 1987/1993 on, non-fiction 2001 on, biography and autobiography in 2005/2006. He wrote his plays in 2010 and operetta libretto in 2012. He painted a series of phthalo blue watercolors entitled *Study in Blue* in 1999. After studying classical piano for ten years, Mr. Lindgren played as a *virtuoso* in May of 1987. One day before his twenty-third birthday, on August 4, 1985, he gave the *a cappella* solo *Were You There?*

1982-1984; 1985-1986 Mr. Lindgren majored in German literature at Pomona College where he also studied sculpture, working primarily in *California alabaster*. His sculpture has appeared in three exhibitions. In 1984-1985 he attended the Freies Jugendseminar Stuttgart in Stuttgart, Germany, an anthroposophical arts youth seminar in the German language where he studied speech formation, eurythmy, clay sculpture and other subjects. Some of his sculptures are perfect works of art. He has eurythmy abilities. He is a student of the work of Rudolf Steiner.

In 1982 Mr. Lindgren worked on the bio-dynamic farm Buschberghof in Schleswig-Holstein, Germany. In 1981-1982 he studied German privately. Through his private and college studies, and his experiences

About the Author

in Germany, he achieved proficiency in the language. Some of his poems of note are in German, his favorite language.

As a child and youth, Mr. Lindgren attended Waldorf Schools (Highland Hall in Northridge, California, October 1973-1980; Green Meadow Waldorf School in Spring Valley, NY, autumn 1979). His Waldorf education is essential to his life. In 1971-1972 he lived with his family in Tunis, Tunisia, North Africa.

He has had a variety of work experiences including dishwashing, waiting on tables, clerking in a drugstore, assistant teaching of small children on four occasions, gardening, student grounds work, work as a farmhand, a handyman, in a hardware store, secretarial work, and production line work in a warehouse. He has tutored math and English. He is conversant in Spanish. He has done translation work from German into English.

Alongside writing, his greatest pleasures include walking, reading German, American, and English literature (particularly anthroposophy, the classics, and poetry), and playing and listening to live classical music. He has sung in eight choirs and enjoyed singing since the Fourth Grade. He is a first tenor with a sweet voice. His favorite music is German baroque religious—especially J. S. Bach—and all folk music.

Mr. Lindgren loves people of all ages. The warm and beautiful sun; the small birds, playful squirrels, friendly dogs, and little cats; the green, blue, purple, and white valleys, hills, and mountains; the bright radiant clouds and sunlight; the colorful blossoms; and the wondrous ocean, moon, and stars, speak to the poet in him. He has a special relationship to the realm of light and color. This is evinced in his love of flowers, the play of light, shadow, and color in the heavens, and painting.

He is a "child of anthroposophy and of the Christian Community." His dearest friends are anthroposophists and priest-pastors. His father Arne Lindgren (1918-1994) was an anthroposophist from Sweden.

Mr. Lindgren lives and works in Los Angeles. His dear Mother lives nearby so that they can visit often.

www.ingramcontent.com/pod-product-compliance
Lightning Source LLC
Chambersburg PA
CBHW051820170626
46807CB00003B/947